PRAISE FOR IRIS MORLAND

PETAL PLUCKER

Funny, charming, and utterly captivating! I devoured this sparkling read.

— ANNIKA MARTIN, NEW YORK TIMES BESTSELLING AUTHOR

Petal Plucker was funny, entertaining, fresh and fan-yourself-worthy . . . Their enemies-to-lovers romance is both charming, tender and steamy, and you'll love both of these characters (and their families!) and their sigh-worthy happily ever after.

— MARY DUBÉ, CONTEMPORARILY EVER AFTER

Morland has created a masterpiece of a romance . . . one of my favorite [books] of the year.

— CRISTIINA READS

Humorous, raunchy, and refreshing, Petal Plucker has rightfully earned its way, in my opinion, as one of the best romantic comedy [books] this year.

— CAROL, TIL THE LAST PAGE

My One and Only

This book was gripping, well written & the chemistry between the characters sizzled throughout this wonderful read.

— AMAZON REVIEW

All I Want Is You

Another heartfelt, steamy, terrific story. This is an author who really knows how to create a story that catches a reader's attention and characters that capture her heart.

— BOOKADDICT

TAKING A CHANCE ON LOVE

Thea and Anthony are in for a surprise when it comes to the language of the heart . . . I am in awe.

— HOPELESS ROMANTIC BLOG

Then Came You

This story really pulled all my heartstrings. This was truly a beautiful story and makes you believe there really is true love out there.

— MEME CHANELL BOOK CORNER

Someone to Watch Over Me

Till There Was You

I'll Be Home for Christmas

HERON'S LANDING

Seduce Me Sweetly

Tempt Me Tenderly

Desire Me Dearly

Adore Me Ardently

TAKING A CHANCE ON LOVE

THE YOUNGERS

IRIS MORLAND

BLUE VIOLET PRESS LLC

For my family. You're the real MVPs.

TAKING A CHANCE ON LOVE

T hea Younger looked over her shoulder to make sure her boss wasn't around and opened a new tab on her Internet browser. She'd already gotten in trouble once before for looking at this website, but she just couldn't help herself.

The photos were mesmerizing; they made her mouth water and her heart pound faster. Her body heated with anticipation as she paged through the photos, one after another, already knowing what she'd see but needing to take them in just one more time.

Who knew that looking at trees could be such a turn-on?

"Whatcha doing?" Nicole, Thea's fellow administrative assistant at the law office where they both worked, asked. She chuckled when she spotted what Thea was doing. "Are you looking at that cabin *again*?"

Thea sighed happily. "Isn't it gorgeous? I'll be there in three days, Nicole. Only. Three. Days."

She paged to the photo that showed the inside of the cabin, which featured an expansive fireplace and high ceilings made entirely of gorgeous oak. Thea had wanted to stay at one of the Mighty Pine cabins for over two years now. She'd finally been able to reserve one of the cabins a month ago, and she would be staying up in the Cascades all by her lonesome for two weeks.

Nicole sighed. "Honey, we need to get you a date if you're drooling over pine trees for the thousandth time this week. What's so great about this place, anyway? It's not like Washington doesn't have trees all over the place."

"But it's the scenery. The open air. You can see the stars! Getting away from the city—"

"We hardly live in a *city*—"

Well, Thea couldn't argue with that. They lived in Fair Haven, Washington, which was more aptly described as a small town.

"Doesn't matter, because I leave everything behind me for two weeks." Thea sighed happily.

Right then, Thea heard footsteps. She promptly closed the webpage just as her boss rounded the corner to her desk.

She'd never thought as a kid that she'd grow up to work in an office, bored out of her mind. It was hardly the stuff dreams were made of.

To be honest, Thea had wanted to be a unicorn when she'd been little. Then, when she'd realized that she couldn't exactly get a job as a unicorn, she'd decided to become an artist. At least that way, she could draw unicorns to her heart's content.

Even now, she still wanted to become an artist who actually got paid for her art (although she no longer drew unicorns), but that would also mean showing her work to other people. That was something she still couldn't do.

"Oooooh, he is so hot. Thea, come look at this." Nicole

popped her head over the wall of her cubicle like a ground-hog. "Your favorite guy is talking again."

Thea shouldn't give in to temptation. She had work to do. Receipts to log, schedules to create… just the thought of both of those things made her get out of her chair to hang with Nicole in her cubicle instead. She'd never claimed to be the greatest worker in the world. Besides, the day was almost over.

Thea's lip curled when she saw who was on Nicole's screen: none other than Anthony Bertram, CEO of Bertram, Sons, and Co., the worst company in the history of forever. Not only were they a multibillion-dollar company whose CEO drew an obscenely huge salary, but they continued to do animal testing for their cosmetic and cleaning products even though there was no reason to do so. They basically tortured animals for money. It was disgusting.

Thea hated Anthony and everything he stood for.

"Look at his stupid, smug face," she hissed.

"Shh!" Nicole turned up the volume on the livestream, obviously not caring if they got caught. Such was the lure of the handsome and rich Anthony Bertram.

Thea could admit that he *was* handsome, in a rich, smug, stupid, arrogant, selfish kind of way. His hair was dark, his jaw strong; he had one of those smiles that made a woman all weak-kneed. He clearly worked out, his suits fitting him perfectly, emphasizing his muscular shoulders and wide chest. He wasn't bulky, though, but tall and fit. At the moment, he wore a dark gray suit with a blue tie; his cufflinks winked in the light of the news studio. They probably cost more than Thea's annual salary.

"How has the company dealt with the social media contro-versy?" the news anchor asked Anthony. Thea barely restrained a snort when the perky and busty anchor licked her bottom lip as she asked Anthony the question.

"These things come and go," said Anthony without any change of expression. "There were a lot of misrepresentations and outright lies in that campaign, and unfortunately, these kinds of things tend to spread like wildfire on the Internet. It's best to wait for it to blow over than to address it directly."

"Can you comment on the controversy itself? Will Bertram, Sons, and Co. continue to do animal testing?"

Anthony's lips turned upward, but it wasn't a smile. Not really. It looked like a predator spotting its prey. Thea shivered at that look in his eyes.

"I can't comment on that," he said, "but as we have said in our statement earlier this week, we pride ourselves on the products we sell, none of which contain parabens or toxins and all of which are one hundred percent organic. We were one of the first in the industry to do so."

"Yes, but the allegations against you—"

"Are ludicrous," interrupted Anthony. "It's nothing except unfounded rumors and salacious gossip. I applaud activists who want to make the world a better place, but when doing so hurts other people, who are they saving? Or what are they saving? Nothing. They're only patting themselves on the back for doing what they *think* is right."

Thea turned red with anger at that comment. She wished she could strangle Anthony Bertram through the computer screen. What an arrogant asshole! That viral campaign had been about exposing the truth and showing consumers where their money was going.

Thea would know: she'd been one of the primary people behind the campaign.

It had been her best friend Mittens's idea. Milton Haverford III, more commonly known as Mittens, was always the instigator in their circle, while Thea would take on ideas and make them into reality. This time, though, Thea had come up with original idea of a viral social media campaign against Anthony's company.

Other members of their activist group had soon joined in. The social media campaign against Bertram, Sons, and Co. had grown slowly, and then a huge celebrity had shared the photos of suffering animals—rabbits and rats, primarily—and it had exploded.

Within the last two weeks, Bertram, Sons, and Co. had had to address the allegations, and apparently their stock had plummeted. People were boycotting their products. When Thea had gone to the grocery store just yesterday, she'd seen the company's cleaning products sitting on the clearance shelves, collecting dust.

Seeing that had filled Thea with pride. She'd done that. She'd made a difference. If they kept pushing, Bertram, Sons, and Co. and other companies like it would have to make changes if they wanted to stay in business. Simple as that.

The news anchor began asking other questions unrelated to the controversy, and Anthony looked bored. He checked his watch at one point. *You'd think after everything that happened, he'd at least attempt to be apologetic,* thought Thea.

"God, he's hot," Nicole repeated. She sighed dreamily.

"He's a terrible person," countered Thea.

"We're all terrible people at the end of the day." Nicole rolled her eyes. "Besides, he's rich. Don't tell me you wouldn't ride that train to Pound Town if given half a chance."

Thea scoffed, although to her annoyance, she felt her

cheeks redden. She hadn't ridden anyone to Pound Town in way too long.

"I prefer my men to have morals. Ethics. A conscience," said Thea.

"You mean you prefer men who are boring and you can dump without getting attached? I've known you long enough to know what makes you tick, Miss Thea, dear. And I've seen the dudes you've dated. They're like warm tapioca: pointless and bland."

Thea shoved Nicole lightly, not willing to admit how right her coworker and friend was. So what if she preferred her men to be a little unexciting? At least they weren't *evil*.

"Do you have anything else you'd like to say about all of this?" the news anchor asked.

Anthony straightened his cuffs. "I'd like to address the people who instigated this." He gazed straight at the camera now. "Your actions have consequences and will hurt real people." He didn't say anything else, but those words settled in Thea's stomach like a rock.

They'd done this to help animals and people. How could they be hurting anyone? He was the one at fault here. But was Anthony just posturing, or was there truth in his words?

Thea put that out of her mind. She just had three more days, and she would be on vacation, enjoying the beauty of the woods, the open air, and not worrying about smug rich assholes like Anthony Bertram.

~

ANTHONY BERTRAM, billionaire CEO of Bertram, Sons, and Co., was having a very bad day.

It had started a few weeks ago. A few innocuous posts on social media—nothing new there. The Internet was a vast cesspool of nonsensical opinions. Anthony never paid attention to people blathering about shit they knew nothing about, especially in regard to Bertram, Sons, and Co.

Until one post had suddenly caught fire and been shared over fifty million times, making the company out to be some evil villain intent on animal torture. Newspapers and blogs and news stations had been calling the company nonstop. And Anthony had watched, rage pulsing through him, as his company's stock had slid down, down, down, and the boycotts against their products had only intensified.

Anthony wasn't about to let some hippie freaks who conflated animal testing with actual torture destroy what he'd built. He would go down fighting, and by God, he'd take those bastards down with him, too.

By midmorning, Anthony already had a headache. He'd been dodging email after email, phone call after phone call, about this PR nightmare. His board wanted a meeting immediately to discuss what to do.

Anthony was already on edge when Bruce Weaver came barreling into his office. Bruce was a member of Anthony's board and one of his first shareholders. Although they'd once had a respectful business partnership, things had soured after Anthony had fired Bruce's son Ryan a year ago. Anthony hadn't regretted the decision one bit, but Bruce had made a point to make Anthony's life hell as a result. This new development had given Bruce plenty of ammunition.

Anthony motioned for Bruce to sit, a thoroughly ironic gesture. "You wanted to discuss something?"

Of course Bruce would just come barging into his office,

as opposed to sending a reply to Anthony's email like a normal person.

"Once again, I would advise you to do nothing about this kerfuffle," said Bruce, ignoring Anthony's invitation to sit. "You'll be making a huge mistake by giving these people the satisfaction of being noticed."

"Considering I've already talked about it in the media, I fail to see how another interview would hurt."

"You think you know everything, don't you? You may be the CEO, but that doesn't make you a dictator, either. You're going to hurt this company irrevocably with your actions."

"And I say that the current strategy is the reason why we've lost millions already."

Bruce pointed a finger at him. "Don't think that you're immune, Bertram. The same people who made you CEO can take you down. Remember that."

Anthony didn't rise to the bait. Shrugging, as if Bruce had just suggested they go golfing, he replied, "Do as you wish. You aren't the board."

Bruce scowled before marching out of Anthony's office.

Anthony's assistant Cara, whose desk was right outside Anthony's office, stood up when Bruce stormed out. Her eyes widened.

Coming to stand by Anthony's door, she opened her mouth, ostensibly to ask a question, when he cut her off. "Has *Society* sent over the draft yet for the article?"

"Oh, oh, yes. They just did," she stammered.

"Send it over. I want to get this out."

Cara was smart enough not to comment on Anthony's choice to continue against what the board—aka Bruce—

thought the PR strategy should be. *If Bruce wants me out, then he'll have a hell of a fight to get there*, Anthony thought.

After Anthony, Bruce held the most shares in the company, but Bruce would need more than half the board to agree before they could vote Anthony out. Bruce would have an uphill battle to manage that particular coup.

Anthony was just glad that he was going away from the city for a while very soon. He'd rented a cabin up in the woods months ago before all of this had started. He was tempted to leave right now, and hell to everyone who thought they knew better than him how to run his own company.

It was late in the afternoon when Anthony's office door opened. "Have you heard of knocking?" he barked, thinking it was another rogue board member.

"Is that any way to greet your ex-wife?" a dulcet voice asked.

Anthony smelled her floral scent before he saw her. He'd always know that scent. Elise still wore the same perfume he'd bought her for their first wedding anniversary even though they'd been divorced for two years already. Anthony had a feeling she did it simply to irritate him.

This shit day's going from bad to worse, he thought sourly. He didn't get up at Elise's entrance, and he didn't offer her a seat, either. She didn't deserve the courtesy.

Cara burst into his office. "Mr. Bertram, I'm sorry, I told her you were busy—"

"I'm sure you did," he interrupted. "Cara, please close the door behind you."

When his office door closed with a click, Anthony returned to the documents on his desk, not remotely interested in giving Elise the attention she craved. If she wanted something—which she most certainly did—she would have to tell him herself.

He heard her sit down across from him in the same seat that Bruce had refused to use. *Why is today the day everyone seems intent on bursting into my office?* he thought darkly. He X'ed out some numbers on the paper in front of him with a bit more force than necessary.

Elise clucked her tongue at him.

Glancing up, Anthony couldn't help but notice that despite everything, she was still beautiful. Damn her.

Wearing an emerald-green dress that showed off every curve yet somehow remained demure, Elise exuded sex appeal in a deceptively simple package. She never wore red lipstick—only pinks and pale plums. She preferred to put her hair up rather than leaving it down, the honey-colored strands soft as silk and the color completely natural. Her sweet façade had been what had attracted Anthony in the first place. It had only been later that he'd seen her capacity for inflicting pain.

"Is this how you treat guests?" she asked, amused. "I thought I'd taught you better manners than that."

He set his pen down and waited, a dark eyebrow raised. Like he'd thrown down a gauntlet, Elise then set her purse, a small clutch with gold trim, on his desk. Anthony knew that he hadn't bought her that purse, so Ryan must have. The thought made him want to punch Ryan Weaver all over again.

Not because Anthony still loved Elise. Far from it. The moment he'd caught her cheating on him with Ryan, who also happened to be his former vice president and best friend, his heart had turned to stone. He'd divorced her before she could explain why she'd decided screwing his then–best friend had been a good idea. No, he'd hated that the two of them had made him look like a fool, that they'd conducted their affair right under his nose.

He would never let anyone make a fool of him again.

He couldn't help but notice the giant diamond on Elise's finger along with the wedding band. She'd gotten Ryan to marry her quickly, that was for sure.

"Why won't you answer my texts? I've texted, called, emailed. Is your phone dead?" asked Elise. She pushed her bottom lip forward in a pout.

Anthony laughed darkly. "I hate to break it to you, but I was ignoring you. Now, unless you have something you actually need to tell me, get out. I have work to do."

To his immense annoyance, she laughed. "You're such a brute, Tony. You always were." Her eyes sparkled.

He gritted his teeth at the sound of her calling him Tony. She was the only one who'd ever used that name with him, and now hearing it on her lips only made him hate her more.

"You always were terrible at compliments," he said.

"Only because you're worse at them," she countered. Probably realizing his patience was at an end, she said, "I want more money, Tony."

He snorted. "Of course you do. The thousands I paid you already to keep your mouth shut wasn't enough?" He gestured toward the giant ring on her finger.

She flushed, covering her left hand. "You know very well that your lawyer screwed me over, and it's not enough to support me." Her voice was stiff to the point of sounding prissy.

"Ryan doesn't give you money?"

She stiffened. Anthony hadn't meant to bring up her latest husband, but with Elise, his self-control tended to dissipate.

"He doesn't give me money because he's still out of work. Because of you." Her eyes narrowed. "I want more money."

"Or what? You'll fuck another man while we're married?" Anthony sneered. "Wait, you already did that."

Elise's cheeks turned bright red. "You ass," she hissed, standing and grabbing her purse. "This is why I left you. You're heartless. A brute, less than human—"

"I distinctly recall that I divorced *you* after I found you naked in our bed. With another man."

The memory of that moment had forever seared itself onto Anthony's mind. He pushed the memory away, refusing to allow Elise to sink her claws into him again.

"I want more money, or I'm going to the press and telling them everything," she said.

Slowly standing up, Anthony rounded his desk and towered over Elise. "You wouldn't dare," he said silkily. "You don't have the balls to ruin your reputation like that."

"Do you want to chance it?"

Her voice wavered, and he knew she was bluffing. Disgusted, he pointed to the door. "Get out of my office. If I see you in my building again, I'll have security toss you out."

Her spine went ramrod straight. "Fine. You'll be hearing from my lawyer, then."

Anthony didn't even flinch when Elise slammed his office door behind her.

CHAPTER TWO

Thea shivered as she peeled off her sodden jacket, trying to find a light switch inside the darkened cabin. The rain continued to fall, pounding on the roof above. Thea finally gave up on trying to find a light switch and turned on her phone to use as a flashlight. Her bladder was about to explode, and it didn't care one bit if she couldn't see to find a bathroom.

Luckily there was a bathroom with just a toilet and sink on the first floor. After relieving herself, Thea ventured into the kitchen. She switched on the oven light, which provided enough illumination that she could get a better idea of her surroundings.

It was close to midnight. She'd planned on arriving earlier in the evening, but a late start coupled with a rainstorm that had turned the twisty forest roads into mud had slowed her down considerably. She'd almost thought about turning back, but her four-wheel drive SUV and her own stubbornness had forbidden her.

Her stomach growled, although fatigue pressed on her

more than hunger. She wanted to crawl into bed and sleep for an entire day. Why was it that sitting on your butt in a car was so exhausting? Yawning, she went and brought in the groceries she'd brought with her and began to put them away.

It took her a long moment to realize that there was already food in the fridge. And food on the counter. Thea frowned. Had Ted, the cabin owner, not cleaned up after the previous people? Considering she'd had to put down a deposit in case she trashed the place, that hardly seemed fair.

She wrinkled her nose when she saw that whoever it was had left breadcrumbs all over the counter. And was that deli meat in the fridge? *Gross.* She threw it into the trash along with some cheese, mayo, and everything else she never, ever ate. *Good riddance.*

After she'd put her food away, she wandered into the living room. She finally found a light switch, and when she flipped it on, she saw that there were books on the side table. She frowned. The books were all boring nonfiction tomes about economics, which sounded like terrible choices to provide your guests. Or the last guy was the most boring person ever and had left them behind.

It was when she saw the boots by the front door that she froze. They were huge compared to hers, so clearly they were men's boots. She crouched down to inspect the boots, and her blood turned cold when she touched the mud on the boots and found it wet. If the mud was still wet, then the wearer had been outside fairly recently. And if the wearer had left them here within the last few hours or so…

She stifled a scream when she heard footsteps upstairs.

Oh God, what the hell? Who would be out here in the middle of nowhere?

Thea's mind whirled, her heart pounding so fast that she felt dizzy. What if some serial killer had come to kill her? But then why leave his stupid boots right there for her to see them? *Maybe he knows it doesn't matter once he slashes my throat.*

She'd unconsciously moved backward toward the kitchen, when she heard footsteps at the top of the stairs. Her heart seized in her throat. If she ran out the front door, he'd hear her and if he caught her—

Sprinting as quickly and quietly as she could, she grabbed a butcher knife from the knife block in the kitchen before hiding inside the pantry. Her only hope was that the intruder didn't notice her things everywhere. Or at the very least, he wouldn't think to open the pantry door.

Thea held her breath when the kitchen light turned on. She heard the fridge door open and then the intruder muttered something. She frowned. Why was he rifling around in the fridge?

"What the hell?" a male voice said.

Thea heard his footsteps depart into the living room, but to her horror, he returned to the kitchen. She clutched the knife. She could call 911, but she was so far away from civilization that once the cops showed up, she'd be long dead, her body thrown into the nearby creek.

Oh God, this was supposed to be a relaxing vacation!

When the pantry door was thrown open, Thea screamed and launched herself at the intruder. He yelled, surprised, pushing her off him before grappling with her. The knife clattered to the floor. As the intruder held her still, she looked up into the eyes of the man who was going to kill her.

And when she recognized him, she was so shocked her voice failed her.

It was Anthony Bertram.

She gaped up at him, her mouth opening and closing like a fish. He frowned down at her like some ferocious predator. He was significantly taller than her, as she only came up to his shoulder. His grip was firm to the point of hurting, but she hardly felt it. Was this some kind of bizarre nightmare? Had he found out what she'd done and decided to kill her himself? But why drive out here to do it? Her mind raced as she started shaking.

"What the *fuck* are you doing here?" Anthony demanded in a voice like thunder. Thea flinched. He continued, "Why are you hiding in the goddamn pantry? And more importantly, *who are you?*"

If he wanted to kill her, he would've done it already. Realizing that she wasn't in any actual danger, she inhaled, trying to find the words to explain.

And then, to both their surprise, she started laughing.

Anthony let her go like she'd thrown acid on him. Thea kept laughing, knowing she sounded like a lunatic and not caring. It was so ridiculous, and she was so jacked up on adrenaline, that laughing was the only way she could calm herself down.

Anthony just stared at her, and it only made her laugh harder.

"Oh my God," was all she could keep saying. "Oh my God, you scared the shit out of me."

"I scared the shit out of *you?*" He shot her an incredulous look. "What the hell are you doing here? I've rented this cabin for me and me only. Are you homeless?"

At that question, Thea's laughter faded. She was wearing

old sweats and her hair needed a good wash, but she hardly looked *homeless.*

"You've rented this cabin? I think you've made a mistake. I've rented this cabin for two weeks. So you're the one intruding," she said.

Anthony shook his head, his jaw clenching. She couldn't help but notice that her nemesis was even handsomer in person: his jaw was practically cut from marble, his hair dark as the night outside. His eyes were dark, too, although if she looked more closely, she could see specks of gold in them.

Not that she was looking. No way.

And then she realized he wore nothing but boxers. She'd been so terrified that his near nakedness just hadn't registered. Her face heated as she took in his muscular torso, his chiseled abdomen and pectorals. His chest was covered in dark hair, while more dark hair pointed straight down to the waistband of his boxers.

She swallowed, mouth dry. As if he'd known she was ogling him, Anthony just crossed his arms and raised one dark eyebrow.

"Who. The. Hell. Are. You?" he asked slowly, raking her with his gaze. "If you aren't homeless, then why the fuck are you in my cabin?"

Thea sighed. The adrenaline leaving her system made her feel shaky, and it was difficult to put the threads of all of this together. And it didn't help that Thea didn't know if she should tell Anthony her name. What if he knew exactly who'd started that campaign against his company?

She had no idea how they'd know—she and Mittens had been careful—but Anthony had contacts and money. That alone should make her wary. Then again, if they did know, he would've sent his lawyers after her already.

But his angry gaze told her he wasn't about to let her keep silent. Deciding to stick with the truth, she said, "My name is Thea. And who are you?" She knew who he was, obviously, but she wasn't going to give him the satisfaction of her recognizing him.

"Anthony Bertram. Now my next question," he said as he went to the fridge and opened it. "Where the hell did all of my food go?"

Anthony had come downstairs to have a midnight snack because he couldn't sleep, only to find a damn crazy woman in the kitchen. He still wasn't totally convinced she wasn't going to stab him. But considering she was half his size and hadn't tried to stab him a second time, he had a feeling she'd been as surprised as he'd been.

The knife on the floor gleamed up at him. Picking it up, he sent Thea an ironic glance. He placed the knife back in the knife block and once again gestured to the fridge. "What happened to my food?" he asked again. Because really, he'd come downstairs for something to eat, and his food had disappeared. Had she eaten it all while he'd been upstairs?

She said, "That's what you're worried about here? Your deli meat that's filled with sodium and that will make your heart explode someday?"

Oh God, she was one of *those people*. He groaned, shutting the fridge. His appetite had disappeared, anyway. He needed to get this woman out of the cabin. Right now.

She was crazy, yes, but when she'd launched herself at him, he'd felt that she was a pleasant armful of womanly curves. She wasn't his type in the slightest: her hair was too short, she had a septum ring in her nose and a sleeve of tattoos all along her right arm. She was also obnoxiously short. He preferred women tall enough that he didn't get a neck ache from kissing them.

Not that he *wanted* to kiss her. He didn't kiss crazy.

He'd driven up to the cabin earlier that day, looking forward to being alone for the next two weeks. Amid the PR fiasco, he'd forgotten about his reservation until Cara had reminded him. He'd considered canceling, but he didn't want to give Bruce and the other members of the board the satisfaction. Bruce would see it as weakness, would think he'd gotten to Anthony.

Anthony would still be working anyway—that couldn't be avoided—and he'd made certain that the cabin he had chosen had reliable Wi-Fi. Besides, Cara was a phone call away, and he could get back to Seattle within three hours if all else failed.

Leaning against the kitchen counter, Anthony crossed his arms. "How about you explain why you're here?" he said. First, he needed to take care of this woman.

"Because I'm renting this cabin for two weeks." Her expression turned mulish. "So why are *you* here?"

Pulling out his phone, he brought up the email from Ted, confirming his reservation. "You must have gotten the dates mixed up." He showed her the email.

But to his dismay, she pulled out her own phone—one with a cracked screen that he could barely read off—and he read that she'd gotten the same confirmation email. *You're confirmed for the Peaceful Waters Cabin at Mighty Pine, April 3–17.* They were the exact same dates as in his confirmation email.

He thrust her phone back at her. "Then there's a mix-up. I'll call Ted in the morning, get you a refund." He wanted to wring Ted's neck. How could he have let this happen? Who booked two strangers at the same time?

"Why should I leave?" Thea countered. She mirrored Anthony by crossing her arms, which only made her small breasts more obvious. He decided to ignore that. "I have as much of a right to stay here as you. Besides, you're rich. You can go anywhere. I've saved up for this trip, while I'm sure this is just a drop in the bucket for you."

"Who says I'm rich?" he said, despite it being completely true.

"Because you have the face of a rich douche, and you're wearing an expensive watch. Pretty easy to guess everything else."

"I'll have to do something about being so obvious."

He called Cara, needing to get this sorted out. Cara was used to getting phone calls at all hours of the night. If anyone could get this crazy woman a hotel room or find a new cabin for her, it was Cara.

"What are you doing?" Thea demanded.

Anthony ignored her.

"Cara, there's a situation. I need you to find me a hotel room for tonight. Somewhere near the cabin. Yes, tonight. No, it's not for me—"

Before he could hear Cara's reply, Thea took the phone out of his hand and ended the call. Anthony stared down at her, immense irritation filling him.

"Give me my phone back," he said in the same tone of

voice he used with people he was ten seconds away from eviscerating. The same voice that made employees quiver in their boots. He'd made more than one intern cry when he'd used this particular voice.

Thea, however, didn't look like she was going to burst into tears. She merely tipped her chin up in defiance.

He towered over her and slowly began to force her backward until she bumped into the wall. So close to her, he could smell her—something citrusy yet also spicy—and he could see that her eyes were a dark grayish green. He was so close that only an inch or two separated them.

She'd put her hands behind her back, the phone still clutched in her grip.

"I'm not leaving," she said with obvious bravado. "I have as much a right as you to be here. I paid for my reservation. I'm not going to let you ruin my vacation."

Anthony smiled, but there was no humor in it. "I don't give two shits what you paid for. I don't care if you're the goddamn queen of England. I've wanted to be alone in this cabin, and I'm not about to have some crazy hippie woman ruin that."

Thea bristled. "I'm not crazy."

"You tried to stab me."

"I thought you were going to kill me!"

"I'm seriously considering it now."

She didn't waver, and Anthony couldn't help but be impressed. Most women would've started crying already. Elise certainly would have. She used tears like a soldier used a gun, and she could employ it at the most opportune time to get what she wanted.

He reached to get his phone, but Thea pushed it higher up

her back. He'd have to turn her around and rip it from her grasp, which meant touching her again. He wasn't going to touch her a second time.

"Give. Me. My. Phone. Back," said Anthony through clenched teeth.

"I will if you promise not to kick me out."

"No."

"Then we'll stay here all night."

He placed his hand on the wall above her head, effectively caging her in. Her chest rose and fell, and he could tell she wasn't as calm as she'd like him to think.

"I have all the time in the world," he said softly. "And I never lose."

Since intimidation wasn't going to work, Anthony decided that he'd try another tactic. There was always something that caused a person to let down their guard. Fear, greed. And lust. Trailing his fingers down her arm, he encircled her wrist. He brushed the soft skin there with his thumb. When Thea shuddered despite her best efforts, he exulted.

"If you're going to stay here," he murmured, his mouth near her ear, "then you might as well give me a good reason to let you stay."

She froze. He stroked her forearm. Then she shuddered.

When he raised his head, his gaze landing on her rosy mouth, he suddenly wanted to kiss her. Right then and there.

Thea licked her lips.

And then a sharp pain radiated from his foot, and he swore as Thea ducked under his arm. She'd stomped on his fucking foot, the little bitch!

She laughed at his pained expression. If she'd broken his foot—

"I'm not going anywhere," she said and ran upstairs, his phone still in her hand. When he heard a bedroom door shut with a bang upstairs, he knew he'd been beaten.

He swore, long and low.

Thea might have won that battle, but by God, he'd win this fucking war.

CHAPTER THREE

Anthony woke up the following morning to the sound of rain against the cabin roof and an ache in his foot. It took him a moment to remember what had happened last night. Namely, that this Thea person had stolen his phone and had stomped on his foot so hard that when he looked at it in the morning light, there was a nice-sized purple bruise on it.

He grumbled, his stomach also grumbling. Thea had locked her door and refused to come out, and Anthony had decided to let her win—this time. Although he was pissed enough to break down her door if he had to.

After a quick shower and shave, he ventured downstairs. He smelled something cooking, and when he went into the kitchen, he found Thea singing as she cut fresh fruit. She also wore tiny shorts with the most ridiculously tight tank top, which only increased Anthony's irritation. Why couldn't she be anything but an attractive woman with an ass that was totally distracting? He wished she smelled like anchovies and never brushed her teeth.

"You're still here," he said flatly. He moved past her to the fridge to find that his missing food had been restored. He grunted. Pulling out some bacon and a carton of eggs, he cracked some eggs for an omelet. He wasn't a great cook, but he could feed himself if he had to. Normally his cook would make him his meals, but just because he was rich didn't mean he was helpless.

Thea ignored him, continuing to sing. Her singing voice was nothing amazing, although at least it seemed to be on key, he thought sourly. She placed fruit in a glass bowl and turned to the stove, pouring what looked like pancake batter onto a griddle. Anthony's mouth watered at the scent.

But more importantly, he needed to get his phone back. Shooting Thea his most intimidating glare, he said, "Give me my phone back."

"Most people say 'good morning' when they first see someone in the morning," she replied in a sugary voice.

"It isn't a 'good morning,' because you're still here and you've stolen my property." He tore open the bacon package, and to his immense delight, Thea's expression turned green at the sight. "You want some?" he taunted.

"I don't eat dead animals. Can you cook that after I'm done?"

"No, because I'm hungry." He found a skillet and set it on the stove next to Thea's pancakes.

She stood next to him now, and as he heated oil in the pan and was about to place the bacon in, she said, "Fine. I'll give you your phone back if you wait until I'm upstairs. Deal?"

He grinned and flipped off the burner. "Deal." He put out his hand, and she pulled the phone from her back pocket. He hadn't thought those shorts were remotely big enough to allow her to keep his phone in her pocket. Electricity danced along his veins at the realization that his phone was warm from her body.

Thea sniffed and returned to her pancakes. Anthony opened his emails, grimacing at how many had landed in his inbox just since last night. Thankfully, there was nothing urgent, although Cara had emailed, texted, and called, concerned about why he hadn't called her after Thea had hung up on her.

He ignored Cara's messages for now. He had something more important to get to the bottom of. He needed to call Ted and figure out this damn mess.

Anthony tapped his foot as Ted's line rang and rang. Finally, he picked up.

"Ted, finally. This is Anthony Bertram. Are you aware that you've booked the Peaceful Waters cabin for not only myself, but another person?"

"What? I'm not sure I understand. You want someone else to come up to stay with you?"

Anthony gritted his teeth. "No, I'm saying that there's another person here who says she has booked the cabin at the same time as me. Her name is Thea. Ring a bell?"

Ted inhaled, and Anthony heard papers being shuffled. Then Ted barked in the background, "Marjorie! Marjorie, where are you!" His voice rose with every word.

Ted returned to the line. "Mr. Bertram, I am so sorry. I don't know what happened. There must have been a mix-up. Marjorie is in charge of finalizing reservations. Let me find out what happened, and I will make this right."

Anthony wasn't interested in waiting. Hearing Thea come into the living room, he said, "I booked this cabin months ago.

This is unacceptable. Make it right, or you'll never do business again. Understood?"

Ted stammered something and promised to get to the bottom of things before Anthony ended the call.

He was about to call Cara when Thea said behind him, "Was that really necessary?"

He turned to see her holding a plate of food. His stomach grumbled from the sight. "This isn't just some tiny mistake. They've fucked up everything because somebody is completely incompetent. So, yes, it was necessary."

"Sometimes mistakes happen. It's life."

"Mistakes don't happen for people like me." He walked toward the kitchen, pausing next to her for a moment. "Enjoy your meal. It's the last one you'll have here in this cabin."

"That sounds ominous. Are you actually going to kill me now?"

"Like I said last night: I'm considering it."

She stabbed a bite of her pancake with a wide smile. "Even rich assholes like you don't want homicide on their hands. Bad PR, don'tcha know."

Anthony stilled at that word, but Thea only bit into a piece of pancake like she hadn't said anything of note. Did she know about his company's PR disaster? Then again, how could she? She hadn't known who he was last night.

"My assistant will find you a hotel room," he said brusquely. "You'll be leaving by this afternoon."

"In this weather? Did you look outside?"

He hadn't, and when he glanced out the window, he saw rain. So it was raining in the Pacific Northwest. That wasn't exactly a deterrent for anyone from around here.

"Unless you're actually a witch, you won't melt in the rain," he said.

"Funny. But apparently there are mudslides everywhere. Actually…" She set her food down and went outside without another word.

Annoyed, Anthony followed, not sure why he cared. The rain pounded down, and both he and Thea gazed upon a driveway that had turned into a sea of mud. Water streamed away from the house toward the bottom of the hill. Based on the clouds overhead, the rain wasn't going to let up anytime soon.

"I can drive in rain, but I'm not about to get swept away in a flash flood," said Thea.

"Then I'll call in a helicopter. I know people."

She gaped at him before bursting into laughter. "Are you serious? That's ridiculous. And where would a helicopter land in the woods?"

"They'd figure it out if I wanted them to."

Thea laughed again, shaking her head. Anthony gazed out onto the rainy landscape, his stomach sinking. If the weather continued, this could get very, very bad. Gripping the door frame until his knuckles turned white, he pulled out his phone and started making calls.

DESPITE HER LAUGHTER, Thea was fuming. She imagined all sorts of terrible scenarios that ended in Anthony Bertram's doom: falling off a cliff, getting run over by a tractor. Being sucked into quicksand. Was there quicksand in Washington

State? If not, she'd go find some and bring it back and toss him into it.

At the moment, Anthony was making *very important* phone calls. His voice had returned to its usual haughty tone, and the only satisfaction she received was hearing his frustration. When he caught her looking at him, he sent her a sardonic glance and headed upstairs.

She speared a bite of pancake, now cold. She hoped he tripped on the stairs.

He was going to get rid of her, was he? Not fucking likely. She would tie herself to the fridge before she let him throw her out. She had just as much right to be here as he did. And she wasn't in the position to go on vacation whenever she wanted to. *Rich assholes are the worst,* she thought as she finished her cold pancakes.

Thea poured herself a cup of coffee and added some coconut milk creamer to top it off.

If she was going to stay here, that meant she'd be stuck here with him. Did she really want to spend the vacation she'd been desperate for with Anthony Bertram, the man she loathed? The man who would kill her if he knew about her involvement with that viral social media campaign?

Not that she felt guilty about that. On the contrary. She was absurdly proud of how she, Mittens, and their friends had gotten the word out and how quickly the posts had gone viral. If they weren't something that resonated with people, why would millions have shared the posts?

Thea headed upstairs. She heard Anthony bark something into his phone. She felt badly for his poor assistant. She hoped he paid the girl way above her pay grade, because she obviously deserved it.

Shutting her bedroom door and locking it for good measure, she opened the blinds, only to see that it was still raining. Thea blew out a breath. Well, like she'd told Anthony, she couldn't leave in this weather. Even her four-wheel drive would slide right off the twisty, muddy roads into some ravine. Thea didn't really want to die just because Anthony was pissed off at Ted.

Thea sat down at the desk in the corner, pulling out the graphic novel she was close to finishing. A tale of a woman who discovers she has the power to see the future, the story had gotten dark and twisty with each panel that Thea drew. She'd intended this particular story to be one volume, but the story had expanded so much that Thea could see multiple volumes in the future.

Although what did it matter how many volumes there were when Thea couldn't find the courage to show anyone her work? She began to sketch the next page in pencil. She was so distracted, though, that she realized that she'd skipped a necessary panel for that page. Grumbling, she tossed that page into the trash and started over.

Thea had begun drawing seriously in elementary school. Her parents' marriage had been crumbling, and her mother, Beatrice, had been struggling with untreated mental illness for years. Art had become a way to escape. She'd go to her room and draw for hours as she'd tried to ignore her parents' fighting.

When Beatrice had died when Thea was twelve, Thea had had to shoulder much of the responsibility of caring for her younger siblings. Trent, her older brother, had done his part, too, although Thea had taken on a more motherly role. Thea's younger siblings—Ash, Phin, and Lucy—had all been under the age of twelve at the time, too young to take care of themselves much.

Thea had stopped drawing during that time. It had only been when she'd reached high school that an art teacher had taken in interest in her and her work. Mrs. Blake had encouraged Thea to draw and even to enter school art contests. Thea had won a swath of blue ribbons and trophies for her work.

After high school, Thea had attended art school for all of a semester before the bottom had fallen out. At an art show showcasing her work, Thea had proudly shown not only snippets of the graphic novel she'd been working on, but other drawings in charcoal and pastels.

"Do you know who that is?" Anna, one of Thea's classmates, had whispered in Thea's ear.

"No, should I?"

"It's Henry Thatcher! The art critic!"

Thea froze, delight and terror filling her in equal measures. Everyone at school knew how much influence Henry Thatcher had not only in the Seattle art scene, but internationally, too. He could make or break an artist's career with a column only a few sentences long. But if he saw promise? That could be the catalyst to take an artist to superstardom.

Henry was short and bald, and he spoke very little as he perused the students' art. Thea had no idea why he'd deign to come to some student art show. Maybe someone had asked him and he'd done it as a favor?

He stopped at Anna's oil paintings, saying nothing for a long moment. Anna shot Thea a nervous glance. Finally, Henry pronounced, "Good," and nothing else.

Anna inhaled sharply, and when Henry turned to continue on, she did a little happy dance right then and there.

When it was Thea's turn, Henry gazed at each of Thea's pieces in turn. Thea waited—hopeful, scared, but excited. Her work had consistently won awards and honors already. Her teachers rarely found fault in her work.

But everything came crashing down within a second when Henry said, "Nothing about these pieces inspires me. They're very drab and lifeless."

And that had been that.

Thea had been crushed. She'd struggled to draw after that because she could only hear Henry's words in her head with every stroke of her pencil against paper. Her professors were worried about her sudden lack of commitment. She failed to turn in assignments; she stopped going to class. She fell into a dark place, where she would be nothing but the poor kid from a dysfunctional family.

Before her first year of art school had even finished, Thea had dropped out and hadn't drawn a single thing for seven years. But when she'd begun working at Ferguson's law firm, she'd needed an outlet for her boredom and frustrations.

But Henry Thatcher's disparaging words had somehow frozen Thea in time. She'd crafted query letters to agents that she'd never sent. She'd posted her work on a blog but had deleted it an hour later. The thought of sending her work out into the world paralyzed her with terror. She hated that she was such a coward. It was a phobia she'd yet to overcome.

Her phone rang, breaking through her trip down memory lane. "Why are you calling me like some old person?" she answered, smiling.

"Because I'm driving," said Mittens.

"You know you'll get pulled over for doing that."

"Tough titties. You said you needed to tell me something. Did you run into a pack of mountain lions up there?"

"Nothing that intense." She inhaled, messing with her pencil. "There was actually a mix-up. There's someone else here in the cabin, too."

"What? Are you serious? That's bullshit. You paid for that. I hope you kicked her out. Or is it a guy? Wait, is he hot? If he is, don't kick him out. Use him for sex and then kick him out."

"He's not a guy you'd want to sleep with, unless you want to, like, die. Believe it or not, I'm stuck in a cabin with Anthony Bertram. Like, *the* Anthony Bertram."

Mittens gasped, and Thea was worried he'd swerve into oncoming traffic. Mittens made a few more incoherent noises before yelling into the phone, "This is amazing! Oh my fucking God!"

Thea frowned. "But he's an asshole."

"Yeah, I know. But now you have an opportunity to get even more dirt on him. Oh my God, oh my God. I'm going to hyperventilate. I need a paper bag. Thea, you can seduce him and get all of his dirty secrets! We can take that fucking company down!"

"I'm hardly some spy that can seduce a man's secrets out of him."

"You're cute, he's a hetero guy. Heteros have no taste. Use that va-jay-jay for the greater good."

Thea heard what sounded like sirens in the background, then Mittens said, "Oh shit, the po-po is here. Talk to you later!"

Shaking her head, Thea tried to return to her graphic novel, but she couldn't stop thinking about what Mittens had said. Thea wasn't about to seduce Anthony Bertram. She also knew that this was the prime opportunity to discover something about him that could bring him and his evil company down.

A few moments later, Anthony banged on her door. "Thea, I need to speak with you. Right now." He barked at her like she was some lowly soldier in the army. Or worse, like a dog.

She'd needed the reminder that he was a huge asshole. Mittens was right: this was a prime opportunity. She needed to take advantage of it.

"I'll be right there!" she singsonged as she thought, *You're going down, Bertram.*

CHAPTER FOUR

"I've pulled some strings, and my contact has agreed to drive up and get you in his Jeep," said Anthony without preamble when she finally came downstairs.

When he saw the flare of anger in Thea's eyes, he ignored it. She was getting out of this cabin whether she liked it or not. He'd throw her over his shoulder, kicking and screaming, if he had to.

"Are you serious?" she said. "In this weather? This is crazy. Once the rain stops I'll drive out of here myself. Besides, I have four-wheel drive. How is a Jeep going to be better?"

"We have no idea when the rain will stop. According to the weather, it isn't supposed to let up for days. Maybe a week. I'm not prepared to wait."

"And what about *you?*" she countered. "What if you get stranded from the rain?"

He shrugged. "I doubt that will happen."

"Since you're so rich, why not call in your private jet? Or even better, Air Force One? I'm sure you have loads of contacts in D.C."

Each word from her was a barb, but he ignored them all. She could hate him all she wanted.

"For one, you can't land a plane around here," said Anthony. "Secondly, getting a helicopter in this weather is complicated."

She scoffed. "Even for you?"

"Yes, even for me." His ego hated that he couldn't get a helicopter here like he'd thought, and even worse, admitting that fact to this woman.

Thea's lips curled. "I thought you could do anything, Mr. Moneybags?"

"Despite what you might think, I'm not the master of the universe." His voice dripped sarcasm.

"Could've fooled me." Thea sighed dramatically. "What about my car? I need it, you know. I can't just leave it here."

"I'll have one of my guys drive it down when the rain stops."

Her nose wrinkled. Thea wasn't conventionally attractive by any means, but she had the body of a dancer, lithe and tight. The thought of throwing her over his shoulder was way too appealing.

He pushed the thought aside. The last thing he needed was to entangle himself with some hippie woman who would drive him insane within a week.

You want her out of here so you don't touch her, his mind told him.

Okay, so what? He was under a lot of stress, and he was obviously losing his mind a little bit to be attracted to a woman like Thea. If he got rid of the temptation, the problem would be solved.

Simple as that.

Thea just crossed her arms and tapped her foot. "I'm not going. You can't make me."

He heard the steel in her voice, and although it amused him, it also rankled him. Standing, he used his height to tower over her. She just tipped her head up, reminiscent of when he'd tried to intimidate her during their first meeting.

"I can make you," he said in a low voice, "and I will. I promise you that. No one crosses me. *No one.*"

"What will you do? Tie me up and carry me?"

"If necessary."

They stared at each other, the moment lengthening until the tension was palpable. Anthony could just make out her pulse beating in her throat, and God Almighty, he wanted to kiss her right there and taste her skin.

Then a loud boom shattered the moment, shaking the cabin. What the hell?

Anthony followed the sound, but not before telling Thea, "You stay here."

"Hell no." She pushed past him into the rain. Swearing, he followed. He wasn't about to let her fall into a swiftly moving stream or get caught in the mud. He was getting rid of her fair and square, not through some random accident. He was an asshole, but as she'd so sweetly stated that morning, he wasn't much for actual homicide, accidental or no.

They followed the noise that was coming from below the hill where the cabin was situated. The rain fell steady and relentlessly, and Anthony had to concentrate on not getting his boots caught in the mud. With every step, the mud made a squelching sound, and it took twice as long to get down the hill as when it had been dry. He just hoped Thea was strong enough to walk back uphill in this weather, because he sure as hell wasn't carrying her.

The closer they got to the creek that had become a river in the rain, the more Anthony's stomach sank. He realized they were nearing the small bridge that crossed the creek. When they rounded a copse of evergreens, Thea gasped, and Anthony wanted to punch something.

A huge tree had collapsed onto the bridge, essentially breaking it in half. Much of the old, splintered wood from the bridge had been swept away in the creek.

That bridge was the only way down the mountain to civilization. Without it, they were stranded.

There was no way his guy could drive up here to get Thea out. It could be days—weeks—before anyone could get up here to help them. And despite his best efforts, getting someone to rescue them via helicopter was essentially impossible at the moment. Anthony had already talked to everyone he could think of and had gotten the same answer: no way in hell.

Anthony broke out into a cold sweat before anger swept through him. He'd needed this time alone to reorder his thoughts, to get away from it all, to figure out what the hell he was going to do with all of the bullshit that was coming down on him. And now—now he was stuck with this woman who was currently at the edge of the bridge, just inches away from the rushing water below.

Anger turned to panic as he watched Thea lose her balance, her arms flailing as the ground fell away from under her feet. In a flash, he wrapped an arm around her waist and hoisted her up and away just in time.

She cried out in surprise. "What the hell are you doing?" she demanded.

She pushed at his arm, but she weighed as much as a feather. Anthony set her down on firm ground none too gently. His body had heated at the feeling of her against him, and it only pissed him off more. He wiped rain from his face.

"If we're going to be stuck here," he growled, "you can't be fucking stupid. I'm not going to jump into the creek to save you if you fall in."

"I wasn't that close! I can take care of myself."

Her face was red, rain rolling down her cheeks, her hair wet now that her hood had fallen away. One part of him wanted to kiss her into submission. The other part wished she'd fallen in the creek instead.

He put her hood up. "Let's go," was all he said.

When they returned to the cabin, Anthony headed upstairs to dry off, his mind whirling. He didn't know how long he'd be stuck in this cabin with Thea, but by God, he could control himself if he had to. He was Anthony fucking Bertram. He hadn't built his company from the ground up by being a damn idiot. He wasn't going to let himself be distracted by his attraction to a woman who would only bring him down.

He scrubbed at his face with a towel. He'd taken on people who had thought he would only be a failure. His wife had betrayed him with his best friend. He'd had investors that were shady, he'd fired employees who'd tried to screw him over. He'd created his empire brick by brick with his own two hands, not caring who he stepped on as he made his way to the top.

One tiny woman wasn't going to lead to his downfall.

Now that Thea had to stay at the cabin for the foreseeable future, she found herself rather wishing she had left when she could. The thought of Anthony throwing her out had made her stubborn, and now she was paying for it.

She was stuck in this place with this asshole for who knew how long. When would anyone get up here to fix that bridge? It could be weeks.

Just the thought of being in the vicinity of Anthony Bertram for weeks gave her hives.

After they'd returned to the cabin, she'd looked him square in the face and said, "I can't go anywhere now."

And to her surprise, he'd said, "No, you can't." Then he'd ignored her for the rest of the day.

That evening, she came downstairs to smell bacon sizzling. Her stomach turned. She'd been vegan for only a few years now, but she'd quickly found that the smell of meat cooking made her sick to her stomach. It didn't help that she knew firsthand where that meat had come from. She'd seen the animals suffering before being led to the slaughter.

But her own stomach was rumbling with hunger, and, defiant, she went into the kitchen to begin making her own dinner. Anthony didn't even glance up at her. It was like she didn't even exist.

Thea got some veggies from the fridge and began chopping. After putting some quinoa on to boil, she ignored Anthony as much as he ignored her. It was ridiculous, how they were acting, but she didn't care. She hoped he choked on his bacon.

Anthony soon began making a sandwich across from her,

some version of a BLT, she thought. She wrinkled her nose as he piled the sandwich with bacon.

"You're going to have a heart attack eating that stuff," she said.

Anthony picked up the sandwich and took a big bite, chewing loudly in front of her. "Why, are you worried about me?" he asked sardonically after he'd swallowed.

"Not in the least. You should eat some French fries, maybe dip that sandwich in mayo. Because then if you die, I get the cabin to myself like I should have."

He snorted. "Hate to break it to you, sweetheart, but I'm in better shape than you probably are."

"It must help that you don't have a heart in the first place," she said sweetly.

He came closer to her and took another large bite of his sandwich. The smell of the bacon combined with the sound of his chewing made Thea pale.

"You're looking a little green," he said, smiling. "Something the matter?"

Anger flaring, she grabbed his sandwich. She then went to the nearby windows overlooking the backyard. Opening one, she tossed the sandwich outside. It landed right in the middle of a puddle, giving a satisfying *plunk* sound before it began to sink into the mud.

"Did you just throw my sandwich out a window?" demanded Anthony. "Are you fucking crazy?"

"Yes, I am. I'd lock my door at night if I were you." She pushed past him, laughter welling up inside her at the expression on his face.

Two can play at this game, asshole.

"You," he said, his voice low and angry. "You'll pay for

that."

"You don't scare me," she taunted.

"Then that's your mistake," were his cryptic words before he pushed past her and out of the kitchen. Before he left, though, he grabbed a bag of beef jerky from the counter and took a bite of one with a flash of teeth.

As she ate her dinner in the living room, Thea wondered how she could weasel useful information out of Anthony to use against him. Obviously he hated her now, so there was no way in hell he'd tell her a damn thing.

Was she ballsy enough to go through his stuff? She considered. At the moment, she was so angry with him that she could dig through his stuff without an ounce of guilt. The only issue was doing it with him in the cabin.

Thea was in her bedroom later that evening when she heard the shower turn on. Anthony tended to take a shower for at least ten minutes, sometimes longer if he shaved afterward. The only reason she'd paid attention was because she'd wanted to shower last night and he'd taken forever to finish.

Thea glanced at the clock. Then, shutting her notebook, she tiptoed into Anthony's bedroom. The second he shut off the water, she'd hightail it out of there.

His bedroom looked like it had barely been used. A suitcase sat on a table next to the wall, and to her immense amusement, he'd hung up all of his clothes and placed socks, belts, and boxer briefs in the drawers. Everything was arranged according to color.

Jesus, who is this guy? When she saw that one of his polo shirts was Armani, she was half-tempted to spill something on the front in revenge.

But this wasn't about his clothes or how ridiculously anal

he was. She found his briefcase and began to rifle through it.

His laptop was locked with a passcode—unsurprising. Same with his phone. Finding his wallet, she discovered the usual things—driver's license, Social Security card, health insurance, bank cards, credit cards. Some cash, but she was disappointed to see that he didn't carry a pile of hundred-dollar bills in his wallet. Not that she was going to steal from him, but didn't rich guys love to carry around lots of money?

She felt around in the pocket in the back of the wallet, pulling out a business card for some auto shop and then what looked like a folded-up piece of paper. But when she unfolded it, she realized it was a photo of Anthony and some beautiful woman with honey-blond hair. What was even more shocking was that Anthony looked…happy. Anthony, happy? She'd almost say that he looked carefree in the photo. Her eyes narrowed when she saw that something was scrawled on the back corner of the photo: *Anthony and Elise, honeymoon.*

Honeymoon. So he was married, or he had been. She hadn't seen a ring on his finger—had she? Gazing at that photo, seeing his wide smile on his face as he gazed down at the woman, something pinched at Thea's heart. If she were crazy enough, she'd almost think it was jealousy.

Stupid. What did she have to be jealous of?

The water shut off. Heart pounding, Thea shoved his wallet back into the briefcase and returned the case next to the nightstand.

She raced back to her room only a second before Anthony emerged from the bathroom.

Letting out a long breath, she couldn't help but wonder why somebody as heartless as Anthony Bertram kept a photo like that in his wallet.

CHAPTER FIVE

Anthony sat down at his laptop the next morning, coffee in hand, and opened his email to find that the *Society* article had been published online. After reading it, however, he was close to tossing his coffee against the wall.

The moment Anthony Bertram sits down across from me at the upscale French café he chose for this interview, he's all business. He drinks the most expensive espresso drink on the menu, and yes, his suits look like they cost more than my annual salary. I'm pretty sure his cufflinks have diamonds in them, in case you're wondering (I am).

"I built this company from the ground up," he says when I ask him about how he's dealt with this flood of bad press. "I won't let anyone stop me."

When he says that, I know he means it. I'm glad I'm not the one he's set his sights on, because I have a feeling this CEO is not just driven but utterly ruthless to boot.

The article continued, characterizing Anthony as a brutal control freak who refused to listen to any kind of criticism. Despite Anthony stating over and over that Bertram, Sons, and Co. had made great strides in providing natural and safe products, despite his explaining that they were phasing out animal testing, despite everything positive he'd told that damn reporter, she'd chosen to focus on his fucking cufflinks. And how he'd get revenge on anyone who crossed him.

Anthony swore and stood from his chair in a burst of rage. People would see another out-of-touch CEO, too rich to care as he supposedly ignored the downtrodden and the poor, helpless animals. As little bunnies were supposedly tortured, the CEO could only take the time to count his money.

Right on time, his phone rang. "This is Anthony," he said.

"Have you read this article? What did I tell you?" Bruce barked into the phone. "I told you not to do it, and look what happened! This is only adding fuel to the fire."

Anthony's jaw was clenched so hard that he was pretty sure his teeth might crack from the pressure. "The journalist assured me it would be a positive spin. The article I read and approved was not this one. Someone fucked me over."

"You're damn right you were fucked over, along with this company. Again. This is only going to make everything worse." Bruce blew out a frustrated breath. "And now you're in the mountains somewhere when shit is hitting the fan."

"I booked this places ages ago, and I can work here as easily as I can anywhere."

"And yet this article seems to say otherwise."

Anthony stared out the window at the rain, continuing to fall. The backyard was a huge mud puddle. He wondered if his sandwich that Thea had thrown out the window had already disintegrated, or if some clever raccoon had managed to scavenge some of it for its own dinner. It was such a ridiculous thought that it only made him angrier.

"Look, Bertram," said Bruce, "I've been patient with

you, and I've warned you. Another stupid move like this, and I'm going to the board. We can't afford another fuckup."

Although Anthony knew that Bruce would have an uphill climb to get enough of the board to oust him, he also wasn't stupid enough to keep pushing. Bruce had an axe to grind, and he was going to grind it until Anthony was nothing but sawdust.

"I'll fix it," said Anthony before he hung up.

After calling Cara and having her contact every damn newspaper and magazine in the country, Anthony rubbed his temples, a headache creating a ringing in his skull. When the ringing continued, he realized it wasn't in his head. It was coming from down the hall.

He followed the sound to Thea's room. The door was open, but she wasn't inside. He listened; she wasn't in the bathroom, as far as he could tell. The ringing sound continued. Anthony found Thea's phone beneath the mess of covers and turned off the obnoxious alarm. Why set an alarm if you weren't going to be around to hear it?

He couldn't help but notice that Thea's room was a mess: clothes strewn everywhere, makeup scattered across a table in the corner. Hair products were on the nightstand, while notebooks covered another table.

His eye was drawn to a colorful drawing. As he approached the table, he saw that the notebook was full of drawings. Not just drawings—some kind of graphic novel?

He began to flip through the notebook. He was hardly some graphic novel enthusiast—he hadn't read a comic since he'd been a kid—but he could see talent in the drawings. The strokes of the pencil, the light and shadow, it all seemed to reflect Thea as a person. When he came to one passage, he even chuckled at the dialogue.

Who would have thought his obnoxious unwanted roommate was a talented artist? He kept reading, immersed in the story completely. The PR nightmare hovering around him disappeared right then as he read Thea's work.

"What the hell are you doing?"

THEA ENTERED HER BEDROOM, only to find Anthony standing at her desk and flipping through her notebook of drawings. A haze of rage and humiliation covered her vision.

No one, not even her family, had seen those drawings. And there he was, looking through them like he owned them.

"What the hell are you doing?" she demanded again as she stalked toward him. She tore the notebook from his grasp before he'd even replied. "And what the hell are you doing in my room?"

"Your phone kept going off," he explained, like he was speaking to a child. "And it was annoying."

"And so you took a detour to look through my things? Do you have any sense of decency?"

He shrugged. Clearly the answer was *no*. "The notebook was open. I saw it, I looked at it. If you didn't want people to see your stuff, maybe don't leave it in plain sight. In case you're wondering, it's good work. And I'm not the type of person who reads that stuff, either."

Thea gawked at him, torn between amazement at his ego and his attempt at a compliment. His arrogance was absolutely astonishing. She'd never met a man so completely unapologetic, so uninterested in giving a shit about other people. When she'd told him that he was lucky not to have a heart, she'd been joking. Now she wondered if she was right after all: the man was heartless—and utterly confusing.

"This is my room. My stuff is private." At that, she winced inwardly. She was the biggest hypocrite. She'd just gone through his stuff yesterday. Swallowing the swell of guilt, she pointed to the door. "Please leave."

Anthony crossed his arms. "Your work is good. You know, most people like when I think they're talented. Most people say *thank you.*"

"I'm not interested in your opinion."

Frowning, he studied her. "You're acting like I was going through your underwear drawer."

Thea blushed. "You're shameless!"

"No, I just hate mysteries. Has anyone seen this novel?" At her silence, he said, "Ah, I've got it. You're—what? Embarrassed?"

"Can you not psychoanalyze me?"

He waved a hand, dismissing her comment. "You have talent that can be monetized. You said before that you didn't have money, so I'm going to guess that you aren't selling your art. Why?"

Thea gaped at him. He'd turned this conversation back on her, and he was too perceptive by half. She wanted to hide under the bed—or stomp on his foot. Both sounded like equally good options.

"Have you ever heard the phrase 'it's none of your business'? Spoiler alert: *it's none of your business!*" she said.

"But why hide it? What's the point of drawing and

creating something if you never share it with anyone else? Isn't that why people do art?"

She hated that he echoed her own thoughts and insecurities, and it only made her angrier. "Like I already said, it's none of your business. None. If I want to draw for nobody but myself, that's my prerogative."

"True. But it's a waste." He plucked another notebook from her desk and flipped through the pages. "I know a number of publishers who would fight tooth and nail to get a hold of this kind of stuff."

The fear that inevitably bloomed inside her anytime she thought of someone looking at her stuff made her blood freeze. Even if some publisher liked her novels, that didn't mean anyone else would.

She heard Henry Thatcher's disdainful voice in her head. *Drab and lifeless.* That was what he'd thought of her supposed talent. And if a hugely influential art critic like Henry Thatcher thought that of her work, who was she to disagree?

She took the second notebook from Anthony's grasp. "What makes you think I care what you have to say about my work? Newsflash: I don't."

"Are you going to toss me out the window like you did my sandwich?" His voice was edged with sarcasm.

"Jesus, you're obnoxious. Are all rich billionaires like you?"

His lips quirked. "Rich billionaire is a bit redundant."

Thea wanted to strangle him, but she forced herself to take a deep breath. "I don't have to explain myself to you or anyone else. I draw for myself. That's it. I don't need to show people my work. I don't need to sell it. I don't need to have it on display for everyone to gawk at and decide if it's worthwhile or not. I don't need everyone to kiss my ass to bring me some kind of happiness. I'm not like *some* people."

"You don't know a damn thing about me. But if we lined up our accomplishments next to each other, we know who the clear winner would be."

"You've just proven my point. You are heartless."

Anthony face creased. She saw something in his eyes that she could almost read as—hurt? That she couldn't believe. She was fairly certain nothing could hurt somebody like him.

He scowled and pushed past her, but not before saying over his shoulder, "If I hear your phone alarm again, I'm tossing the thing out the window."

Thea stuck out her tongue at him like a child before she slammed her bedroom door shut. Burying her face in a pillow, she let out a scream of frustration, imagining all kinds of terrible things happening to Anthony.

After Thea had calmed down, she started looking through her graphic novel. She touched each panel with light fingertips, smiling as she read what she'd already completed. Oftentimes when she finished a draft, she would be convinced it was horrible and unworthy of seeing the light of day. That just meant she needed to let it simmer. She would then come back to it later with a clear head.

Thea knew as she read each panel, looked at each drawing, that her work was good. Great, even. She'd worked her ass off on this graphic novel. When she reached where she'd left off, she sat down at her desk and got to work again.

Maybe no one but herself would ever read this. Maybe she'd never get the courage to query agents or have it published. Maybe she'd have a box of graphic novels, never published, hiding under her bed when she died.

But that didn't mean she couldn't be proud of herself for her hard work. Because if no one cared whether or not she drew, wasn't it almost a greater accomplishment to create something for absolutely no gain?

Anthony could crow all he wanted. Thea knew that at the end of the day, she was still the better person, no matter how much money he had.

CHAPTER SIX

It wasn't until Saturday, an entire week after Thea and Anthony had arrived, that the rain finally stopped. By that point, the entire cabin was surrounded by mud and puddles that resembled small lakes. Despite the mud, when the sun peeked out from behind the clouds, Thea put on her hiking boots and jacket and headed outside.

She and Anthony had avoided each other since their confrontation in her bedroom. They'd barely spoken more than ten words to each other altogether. That was fine with Thea.

She just hoped that now that the rain had stopped, she could get out of here. Her resolve to stay had disintegrated in the face of actually having to be around Anthony Bertram. And despite wanting to find some kind of dirt that she could relay to Mittens, she wasn't exactly going to get results by not speaking to him. Or even getting near him or his things.

Thea sighed happily as she felt the sun on her face. Even though mud sucked at her boots with every step, she didn't care one bit. She could clear her head, take in some fresh air, and maybe figure out how she was going to stay in this cabin with the worst man in existence for who knew how much longer.

Thea's progress was slow as she went downhill, even slower than the first time she and Anthony had come down here. At one point, she got her foot stuck in a particularly sticky patch of mud and had to yank herself free, almost falling on her butt.

Thea wandered to where the bridge had collapsed. It looked worse than a few days ago. Old lumber was splintered in half from the tree that had fallen onto the bridge. The creek had practically turned into a river with all the rain. Thea's stomach twisted at the sight.

She and Anthony weren't going anywhere anytime soon, that was for sure.

Walking parallel to the creek, she let her thoughts wander. Her heart lifted the further she walked from the cabin. She wished she could just walk all the way home and never see Anthony Bertram again.

The night before, she'd caught him coming out of the bathroom in nothing but a towel. She'd frozen, staring at him, deeply annoyed at how damn handsome he was. As if he had known what she was thinking, with his towel hugging him low on his hips and camouflaging nothing, he'd grinned. Thea had stood her ground, refusing to scamper back to her room like a scared little rabbit.

His scent had wafted toward her, spicy and masculine. His hair had curled against his forehead slightly, something so surprisingly playful when the rest of him was so hard and unmovable that Thea wished she could touch that single curl. His cheeks were freshly shaven, but she could still make out the dark grain of his beard. She had a feeling he always had a five-o'clock shadow by the end of the day.

Anthony had brushed past her to get to his room right then, but not before he'd leaned down and whispered, "You're drooling."

A moment later, Thea had slammed the bathroom door shut so hard that it had shaken the cabin.

Thea blew out a breath as she walked. So what if Anthony was handsome? She wasn't dead. She also wasn't going to get her panties damp over a total asshole, either. His kind of arrogance didn't turn her on. In fact, it was a huge turn-off. His handsomeness definitely did not get her panties wet in any way, shape, or form. The thought of kissing him? Disgusting. Totally, completely, absolutely…disgusting.

Except the thought of kissing him sent a shiver through her—and not one of disgust. *Get it together!* she scolded herself. *He probably doesn't even care if a woman has an orgasm or not. It's all about him, no one else. He's an arrogant jerkface.*

Thea didn't know how far she'd walked when she stopped, the creek having narrowed considerably. She glanced at her phone to check the time. Realizing she needed to turn around so she wasn't wandering around in the dark, she headed back to the cabin, following her muddy footprints.

She wasn't far from the cabin when movement caught her attention in her peripheral vision. She squinted: there was a small island in the middle of the creek. Where she was now, the creek was at least one hundred feet wide, give or take. It looked as if an embankment that started from the other side of the creek had essentially become an island from the rising waters. And in the middle of the island was a small animal—a squirrel?

Thea stepped as close to the edge of her side of the embankment as she could. No, it wasn't a squirrel: it was a rabbit. Her heart squeezed when she saw that the rabbit kept going near the edge, as if checking if the water had gone down, only to turn around and try the same thing on the other side. The island itself was only about five feet in diameter. And given how much rain there had been, the rabbit could easily starve to death if it stayed there since there was no way the water would recede anytime soon.

Thea glanced around. The current was too fast for her to wade into it, and who knew how deep it was? She'd be swept downstream before she even got to the rabbit's island.

Frowning, she began to walk toward the cabin, hoping to find some kind of log or way across the stream. Maybe she could return where it was narrower, hop across, get the rabbit, and walk back…

She returned to where the bridge had collapsed and saw that there was enough of a bridge still to make it to the other side. She considered. She took in the bridge, looking to see how safe it would be to walk on. It was probably crazy to do this for a rabbit. She knew that. But she'd always had a soft heart for animals, and the thought of doing nothing for the creature was out of the question.

Thea looked around, her gaze landing on a large rock. When she picked it up, she guessed it was at least fifty pounds. She placed it on the bridge's edge, and when the bridge held, she knew that she had to at least try to get across.

She took one step onto the bridge. It held. She breathed a sigh of relief as she was about to take another step.

But when she took that second step, something cracked under her feet. She felt something shift under her. Frozen with fear, she was about to step back onto land when something hard wrapped around her waist and lifted her into the air.

Thea yelped in surprise as she was pulled against a hard torso just as the part of the bridge she'd been standing on broke and fell into the water. Her heart froze in her chest. That could've easily been her.

Over the sound of her panting, she finally heard Anthony's voice. It boomed in her ear as he said, "Are you fucking crazy? Do you want to die? Didn't I tell you not to get too close?"

His arm was still around her waist like an iron band. He was all hardness, his body tight with tension. If she leaned her head back, it would rest right over his heart. She trembled. Adrenaline made her shaky.

She swallowed, her throat dry. "How did you…?"

"I saw you as I was walking down here. You're damned lucky I was here. You could've fallen in! Do you know how fast that current is? Jesus, the last thing I need is to try to get EMTs up here. Or worse, fish your dead body out of the creek because you've lost your mind."

She looked down to see that his hand was on her hip, his fingers long and brown, the nails filed neatly. His nails were neater than hers. She wondered if he got manicures. He was rich, so he probably did. That thought calmed her.

"You can let me go now," she said, a bit too breathless for comfort. She was too aware of how warm his hand was on her body.

He seemed to hesitate. Thea waited, not entirely sure what she was waiting for. Something like desire bloomed inside her. She almost wished he wouldn't let her go.

He finally came to his senses and let her go. Thea tried to force down her disappointment.

"What were you doing?" Anthony asked again. His expression was irritated, but Thea could see that he had also felt that spark between them when he'd touched her.

If Thea were feeling particularly fanciful, she could almost imagine that he sounded concerned. She pointed. "There's a rabbit stranded on an island in the middle of the creek. I was going to get it."

He stared at her. "A rabbit. You were about to kill yourself to save a rabbit."

Thea's cheeks heated, but she just crossed her arms and shot him a mutinous look. "I tested the bridge," she said, but it sounded like a lame excuse. Trying to explain, she added, "I shouldn't have been so impulsive. I tend to act first, think later. It was stupid of me. But I saw that rabbit and I just—" She shrugged, knowing that he wouldn't understand why it mattered.

He didn't mock her, to her surprise. He just went to the edge of the embankment and said, "Where is it?"

"Why?"

He turned back toward her. "Show me."

Confused by his interest, she tried to figure out his game. Finally, Thea sighed and waved at him to follow her. They walked in silence.

When they arrived at the island, she pointed. The rabbit was currently huddled in the center of the island, looking dejected. It broke her heart.

"It'll starve to death," she explained. Tears burned her eyes. The rabbit had to be terrified, cold, hungry… it didn't deserve to suffer a death like this. At least a predator making it its dinner would give it a quick death. This was just torture.

"I can't just leave it," she said.

Anthony was like a stone wall beside her. She sighed.

"Look, I'll figure something out," she said as she began to walk back to the cabin.

But he stopped her as he said, "Wait. Let's make a plan. Even if you get to the other side, you won't be able to reach the rabbit."

She stopped in her tracks. "What? Are you saying—"

"There's no reason to get yourself killed for a rabbit." Anthony's look was faraway, but calculating. She wondered if that was the look he got as he ran his company. She had to admit, it was kind of sexy.

"So what do you suggest?" she asked, curious, if not wary.

"We need a net. Something to catch it without getting into the water."

Before Thea could reply to that, he started walking back up the hill with a determined stride. Although she was tempted to follow him, she was more interested to see if he would actually come back.

And really, why did he care in the first place? Thea couldn't make out his motives at all.

About fifteen minutes later, Anthony returned with a net, the handle of which was at least three feet long. He'd also changed into different clothes, including a pair of worn jeans and an old t-shirt. Thea couldn't believe he even owned either piece of clothing.

"Where did you find a net?" said Thea.

"The supply shed on the property. There's tons of stuff in

there for fishing and hunting." He placed the net's strap over his shoulder to keep his hands free.

"So you're going to save the rabbit now?" Thea was incredulous. She couldn't believe he was deciding to do something purely out of altruism. Would he demand that she pay him somehow after he'd saved the rabbit?

"The creek narrows down here," he said, pointing. "I can walk across it here, get to the other side, and get the rabbit."

Thea blushed, because it was a much better plan than crossing the bridge.

Where the creek narrowed, it was about thirty feet across.

"Are you sure?" asked Thea. "You don't have to do this."

He shot her a wry look. "No, I don't. But my arms are longer than yours, so you won't be able to reach the rabbit from the other side." He shrugged, like there was no question about him doing it.

"Plus, like I said: I'm not fishing your body out of the water."

"How noble you are," said Thea as Anthony began to wade the creek.

He smiled at Thea's sarcasm, but soon his attention was focused solely on not letting the current pull him further downstream.

Despite the narrowness, it was surprisingly deep, the water reaching to Anthony's knees at one point. He was just glad that he'd brought rain boots with him. Unlike Thea, who had tried to cross the bridge in nothing but tennis shoes. He rolled his eyes.

He didn't know why he was doing this. Maybe it was because when he'd seen Thea step onto the bridge, he'd thought the worst. Had he driven her to do something desperate, if not suicidal? Terror mixed with sheer rage had propelled him forward until he'd plucked her from harm's way for a second time. The woman was bound and determined to get herself killed for some reason.

Of course she hadn't been trying to die—she wanted to save a damn rabbit. Anthony growled under his breath. The woman *was* insane. Who did that?

After their argument in her room, her words had burrowed under his skin like a thorn. *You are heartless.* He'd never disagreed with that assertion. Elise had called him as much since their divorce.

But hearing those words from Thea—soft-hearted, artistic Thea—had stopped him in his tracks. For some reason he didn't want to contemplate, he'd wanted to prove her wrong. He wasn't heartless. He was human, too. He'd loved once, and he'd lost, and she was completely wrong about him.

Anthony hated when people got him wrong. Which was the only reason he could think of why he was crossing the creek to rescue a rabbit. Not because he wanted to prove to Thea that her words had actually wounded him.

He was almost to the other side of the creek now. The current was fast enough that it had taken him longer than he'd anticipated. When he stepped on what was probably a slick rock, he felt his balance slip. He caught himself just in time.

"Be careful!" called Thea.

Anthony waved a hand at her over his shoulder. His heart thumping, he kept moving, and finally, he reached the other side. He blew out a breath of relief.

If anyone could see me now, they wouldn't recognize me. Elise would laugh in my face.

Anthony moved down the embankment to where the rabbit was trapped. He realized that he was a few feet from being able to reach the rabbit with the net. Damn. He'd have to wade into the water here, something he'd wanted to avoid, since the current was faster.

He thought of Thea trying to get into the water here, which would probably reach her waist. A nip of fear bit into his gut.

When he'd said that he hadn't wanted to fish her body out of the creek, he hadn't really been joking.

Thea had followed him along the other side. "Everything okay?" she called.

"Yeah, I'll just have to get into the water, which I didn't want to do. Damn."

The rabbit reacted to their voices, its ears standing straight up. It darted to the side, almost falling into the water before careening back into the center.

From Anthony's vantage point, he could see how much it trembled. The poor thing might drop dead from fear if he weren't fast enough. Then Thea would never forgive him.

Stop caring what Thea thinks of you, he thought.

Getting out the net, he slowly waded into the water. The current pushed at his ankles and then his calves, but he was strong enough not to let it push him over. Reaching with the net, he was able to place it right over the rabbit in a swift motion. The rabbit froze.

Anthony nudged it with the edge of the net, praying that it would venture further into the net so he could lift it up. The rabbit, spooked now, ran headlong until it reached the bottom of the net. Anthony picked up the net, rabbit and all, triumph filling him.

Thea hooted from the other side of the creek. "You did it!"

Anthony was about to let the rabbit go when he saw a dark smear on the rabbit's back leg. The thing was injured. He swore. He couldn't just release it into the woods now. Some predator would catch it by the time the sun set.

"What is it?" asked Thea.

He grimaced. "It's injured. I think something tried to take a bite out of its back leg."

"You can't just let it go, then. Can you get back over with it?"

He didn't want to, but hearing the concern and anguish in Thea's voice gave him a reason to try. He didn't know why this suddenly mattered to him, why he cared about doing this for her. Or was it really for Thea at all? Had he gotten so cynical that he'd convinced himself he wasn't capable of doing something purely altruistic?

He dismissed the idea. He'd done this because Thea was impulsive and she would've gotten herself killed.

Thea said something else, but right then, Anthony concentrated solely on wading back into the water with the rabbit still in the net. The creature was paralyzed with fear now, and Anthony gently twisted the net until he was able to place the rabbit in the crook of his arm. At least this way he'd have one arm free.

Finally, they reached the other side. Thea took the rabbit from him, her expression one of sheer gratitude, something Anthony hadn't seen anyone give him in ages.

"Thank you," she whispered. "Thank you so much."

He grunted, feeling embarrassed, and gestured at her to start the trek back up the hill to the cabin. He ignored how much he liked hearing that tone in her voice, or how she'd looked at him like he was a hero.

Anthony was no hero. If he was anyone in this story, it was the villain. They'd both be better off remembering that.

CHAPTER SEVEN

Thea took the rabbit into her bedroom and wrapped it in a towel to get it warm. She knew that rabbits could die of shock, and she held her breath, hoping the poor thing wouldn't collapse from the stress of its adventure. The fact that the rabbit wasn't even trying to get away said everything. Thea just hoped they hadn't acted in vain.

Anthony knocked on her door. "How's it doing?" he asked.

"It's alive. Actually, could you find me a box or something to put it in?"

Anthony nodded; she heard him go downstairs. She still couldn't believe he'd helped her rescue the rabbit. Where had the arrogant, selfish billionaire gone? The one without a heart? The one who didn't care about testing on animals and sure as hell didn't care about helping other people?

Thea couldn't help but wonder if he had an ulterior motive, but then she dismissed the idea. He had nothing to gain from *her*. In fact, she had more to gain from him in this situation. But he'd crossed the creek, potentially risking his own neck, to save a rabbit. He'd said it was because he didn't want Thea to break *her* neck, but she didn't buy that. At least, she thought that was only part of the reason.

Her thoughts spinning, she didn't even hear Anthony return. He placed a cardboard box filled with newspaper on the floor, along with a plate of various vegetables and a bowl of water. Her heart squeezed at the sight. His actions today weren't helping her to continue hating him.

Thea ignored her own thoughts as she gently placed the rabbit in the box. She kept it wrapped in the towel, although it could free itself if it wanted. The rabbit's nose twitched. It huddled in the corner of the box without moving, although Thea could see the towel shivering.

"I don't know what rabbits eat, but I assume it's the same as what you eat," said Anthony, his voice dry. Then, he said more seriously, "Do you think it'll survive?"

Thea chewed on her bottom lip. "I don't know. I wish we weren't stranded here. I didn't know it was injured. I thought we'd just let it go. I'm hardly a vet."

Anthony peered into the box, not saying anything, although she knew he thought the same thing. All they could do was hope for the best.

He was about to leave when Thea blurted, "Thank you, again. I know you didn't have to help me, but—" She blushed a little. "It means a lot to me."

Anthony looked almost surprised at her words before he shrugged, rubbing the back of his neck. "I'll be in my room," was all he said before he shut the door behind him.

Thea placed the bowl of water in the rabbit's box, along with a few pieces of lettuce and carrots. She smiled when she saw that Anthony had cut up some peppers and…was that cantaloupe? Thea thought she better stick with the lettuce and carrots for now. She could search online what fruits and veggies rabbits liked to eat later.

She watched the rabbit, making sure her room was as warm as she could make it. The rabbit slowly stopped shivering after a while. Thea's heart sped up when she saw it poke its nose further out of the towel. Its whiskers twitched. Thea held her breath. When a noise sounded from Anthony's room, the rabbit returned to its towel burrow.

Thea blew out the breath she'd been holding. "Poor little thing," she murmured.

She hadn't gotten a good look at its injury. She hoped its leg wasn't broken, because she had no way of helping the rabbit if that were the case.

She didn't want to leave the rabbit alone, so she went to her desk to get some work done. Except she couldn't concentrate at all. She could only think about how it'd felt when Anthony had pulled her from the bridge. How he'd taken control of the situation with the ease of a born leader. How he'd caught the rabbit and placed the animal in her arms as tenderly as a newborn kitten.

How could she hate someone when he'd gone out of his way to help her?

Thea had wanted to hate him. He was arrogant; he'd tried to get her thrown out of the cabin without so much as discussing it with her. He'd mocked her, and he'd run roughshod over her. He was the type of person she despised, not to mention that he was the CEO of a company whose standards she believed to be completely immoral.

Bertram, Sons, and Co. represented a cruelty that Thea could never support. It was all about earning money—more money than any one person could ever need—without caring in the least who or what it hurt in the process.

And yet, could a man with no heart rescue a rabbit like that? Thea didn't think so. She thought again of his face when she'd called him heartless. Had she actually hurt him by saying that? She couldn't believe it.

She'd seen a side of Anthony Bertram that she had believed didn't exist, and oddly enough, that was more terrifying than his anger or his selfishness. Because if Anthony was human—if he had a heart—then Thea couldn't tell herself that her actions wouldn't hurt him.

Thea could destroy a monster without guilt.

But what if Anthony wasn't the monster she thought he was?

THAT EVENING, Anthony felt like some kind of caged animal. He was overly aware of Thea's every move: when he heard her open her bedroom door, he came to attention, listening. He even heard her singing as she made herself dinner, which annoyed him greatly.

Why did she have to captivate him thoroughly? She wasn't his type. She was a bleeding heart, and she'd almost gotten herself killed for a *rabbit*. Who did that? People without any brain cells did that.

And since he'd ended up being the one to save the stupid rabbit, he clearly had the least brain cells of them both.

That afternoon, he'd focused on work, taking calls from his team about their strategy going forward. Bruce was still angry—no surprise there—but he'd left Anthony alone since that initial phone call.

Anthony had also spoken to the editor-in-chief at *Society* and chewed him out so thoroughly that he'd probably pissed himself. He'd also assured Anthony that they would write a retraction and an updated version of the article after Anthony had told him exactly how he'd sue him, his family, and the company he worked for. Given Anthony's team of lawyers that had gone after other people and had bled them dry for lesser offenses, the editor-in-chief hadn't been stupid enough to call Anthony's bluff.

But all of that had left Anthony drained and exhausted. He'd come to the cabin because he'd refused to show weakness to Bruce and the board, and he'd refused to give in to Bruce's demands. Now, though, he almost wished he'd stayed in Seattle.

At least there, he wouldn't have to be around Thea Younger.

He groaned as he remembered how she'd felt when he'd grabbed her from the bridge.

He needed to stop touching her, dammit. But he couldn't stop thinking about the warmth of her body, how it was both willowy but strong. Her lemon scent captivated him. She was so short that the top of her head only reached his chin. Yet despite her small stature, she never cowered. There was bravery in her that he'd never seen in a woman. And God Almighty, he wanted to capture it for himself.

Anthony also didn't want to think about the fear that had stopped his heart when he'd seen her stepping onto the damn bridge. Terror like he had never known had frozen him in his tracks. If he'd been a second too late…if he hadn't been out walking at the same time as her…

It didn't bear thinking about.

Anthony rubbed his temples. Her words to him, that he was heartless, had clearly gotten under his skin more than he'd thought. Normally he would've laughed off something like that—he'd heard worse from his own family and from Elise.

Like some kind of bizarre penance, he pulled out the folded-up photo of him and Elise on their honeymoon from his wallet. He didn't keep the photo out of sentimentality; all his feelings for her had dissipated the moment he'd found her in bed with Ryan. No, he kept the photo as a reminder of what happened when he let himself be weak.

Anthony had met Elise two years after he'd started his company, at some charity event where he'd been cozying up to potential investors. Elise had been the most beautiful woman there, and when he'd seen her, he'd known she was his.

Elise Edgerton, the daughter of a senator father and a model mother, had never worked a day in her life. As a socialite and party girl, she'd preferred to spend her time shopping, getting her hair done, and going to parties. Despite her seemingly frivolous ways, Anthony had instantly recognized that Elise was savvy and just as interested in making a mark on society as he was.

That first time he'd seen her, he'd watched her look bored as some old politician had droned on and on. Picking up a glass of champagne from a tray, Anthony had pushed his way through the circle, touching Elise's arm like they'd known each other for ages.

"Sorry for the delay. They had to bring up more bottles of

champagne from the kitchen, apparently." Anthony handed the glass to Elise.

She took it, an amused expression on her face at his audacity. "I was wondering where you were," she replied, her voice sardonic.

"Anthony Bertram," said Anthony as he shook the old senator's hand. Turning back to Elise, he added, "Let me show you that painting I was speaking to you about earlier."

She smiled, made her excuses to the senator, and took his arm. When they were out of earshot, she said, "Do I know you?"

"No, but you will."

"Aren't you a slick one?" Elise sipped her champagne, her red lipstick making a print on the rim of the glass. With her honey-blond hair in loose ringlets down her back, her dress simple and black but with an open back, she looked like a siren. She practically dripped with diamonds, and with every movement, she sparkled.

"Not slick," countered Anthony, "just determined."

"For what?"

As they reached an alcove that offered some amount of privacy, he whispered into her ear, "To have you in my bed."

Elise tittered with laughter. She pushed him away, although it was with a light touch. She let him squire her around for the rest of the party, and Anthony was certain she would return home with him.

But when they went outside, she said, "Call me when you've made it. I don't sleep with nobodies." She handed him her card, smiled like the siren she was, and slipped into the back of a limo.

Anthony's company was up-and-coming then, but he still

wasn't making a profit. He ate ramen noodles; he lived in a dump in the suburbs of Seattle. He barely slept, because all he did was work. Going to this event tonight—and renting a tux—had almost not happened simply from lack of funds.

Anthony had vowed that night that he wouldn't give up. He would have Elise for his own, and he'd be one of the richest and most powerful men in the country. Then the world. The next time he saw Elise Edgerton, she would be his.

Anthony touched Elise's smiling face in the photograph. After Bertram, Sons, and Co. had exploded, Elise had definitely noticed him. He'd transformed into a somebody. When he'd called her up to remind her of her promise, she'd laughed and said she'd wondered when he'd come to collect.

They'd gotten engaged after dating briefly, their wedding the biggest event of the season. And on their honeymoon in Tahiti, he'd been the happiest he'd ever been. He'd thought Elise had felt the same.

He'd fallen in love, and he'd paid for it. He'd vowed to love and to cherish forever, but apparently, Elise hadn't. She'd cheated on him with his best friend and vice president only six years after they'd married.

He folded the photo back up, scowling. He needed to remember what happened when he let his guard down. Letting Thea in would be disastrous.

That evening, he stayed in his room. He hadn't seen Thea since bringing her the box for the rabbit. He assumed she was watching over the animal. He wondered if it would survive. He hoped it would, because the last thing he needed was Thea crying and moping the rest of the time they were stuck here together.

Admit it, you care about her. You want to show her that you aren't heartless.

Maybe he did; maybe he had something prove. So what? He'd done his one good deed for the year. He didn't need to repeat it.

He heard the bathroom door open before the water began running. Realizing she was taking a bath, his mind immediately filled with lurid images.

What would Thea look like naked? He wondered what color her nipples were, if she had freckles on any other parts of her besides the few that were sprinkled across her nose. Mostly he thought about her being wet and slick from her bath, her skin pink, how she'd smell womanly and sweet afterward.

His cock hardened, and he growled in annoyance. He didn't need this right now. Pushing the thoughts aside, he concentrated on important matters at hand. Not on his obnoxious roommate, no matter how much he'd like to see her naked.

An hour later, Anthony got up to go downstairs for a beer, only to run into Thea as she was leaving the bathroom. She had a towel wrapped around her, the ends of her short hair slightly curled from the steam. Her skin was pink, just like he'd imagined, and to his immense amusement, she blushed even pinker as he raked her with a seductive gaze.

She was about to scamper away when he asked, "How's the rabbit?"

"The rabbit?" She blinked. "Oh, um, it's fine. It drank some water, which is good."

Anthony didn't give a damn about the rabbit, not when he could take in Thea standing in front of him, barely clothed.

Her toes were curled under her into the rug, her calves shapely. Her towel barely reached to midthigh, allowing him to see how pale her skin was.

His gaze continued to skim up her body, where she held the towel closed right above her breasts. Her chest rose and fell, only accentuating her cleavage. Her breasts were small, but he had a feeling they were the perfect size to fit in his mouth.

"Good," he said, barely hearing what she'd said.

A few bubbles remained on her neck from her bath. Unable to resist temptation, he reached out and brushed the bubbles away with a soft touch.

Her eyes widened. She didn't say anything, but her eyes said it all. Her breathing quickened, filling Anthony with triumph. She wanted him as much as he wanted her.

"You missed a spot," he murmured.

She licked her lips. Then she met his gaze, her pupils large, her cheeks flushed. Anthony knew enough about women—about seduction—to know when they wanted him. And Thea was giving him all the signals, down to the way her feet were pointed toward him and how she kept touching the ends of her hair and twisting a strand around her finger.

He couldn't help but brush fingers down the slope of her shoulder. She hitched in a breath.

He wanted to kiss her. No, he *needed* to kiss her.

And Anthony wasn't going to stop himself from getting what he needed.

Inhaling the scent of lemons, he tilted her chin back and kissed her.

Thea gasped. He wondered if she'd bolt. He kissed her

softly, letting her make her choice. Finally, she moaned and twined her arms around him. *Thank God.*

The moment their mouths had touched, it was like something inside Anthony shattered. He groaned, deepening the kiss, slicking his tongue against hers. He wrapped an arm around her. Her body, pressed against him, only added gasoline to the fire.

His hand wandered down her back until he could squeeze her ass. She shuddered. She moaned again.

But soon she was shaking her head, pushing him away.

"No, I can't," she said, her voice breathless. She pushed at him again, and although it almost physically hurt to do so, he let go.

Thea touched her lips, her fingers trembling, before muttering, "I'm sorry." She practically sprinted back to her room.

When Anthony heard her lock her door, he flinched.

CHAPTER EIGHT

Thea couldn't stop trembling. It wasn't the cold, considering she'd left her room so warm for the rabbit. And it wasn't even because she wore only a towel.

It was because she'd never been kissed like that. No man had ever kissed her like he would consume her very soul. Anthony had kissed her and, in the process, had imprinted himself upon her like a brand.

She touched her kiss-bruised lips. It wasn't like she was some innocent virgin. She'd had boyfriends, although she hadn't dated much in the last few years, mostly because Fair Haven wasn't great for dating. She'd lost her virginity in high school to her first boyfriend, and she'd enjoyed sex with different men in her early twenties.

But this wasn't about sex. Not really. Oh, Anthony definitely wanted her—she wasn't stupid enough to think otherwise. But that kiss—it had obliterated all of her good intentions, all of the warnings she'd given herself about Anthony.

He wasn't a good man. She knew that. She could list every

reason why he was a terrible, terrible choice for her. She could write a damn dissertation on the subject! And she'd been behind the social media campaign to take down his company. If he ever found out who she really was, he would never forgive her.

Yet he'd saved that rabbit to help her. So who was the real Anthony? Thea didn't know anymore.

Thea got dressed in her pajamas and sat on the floor next to the rabbit. She still needed to name it. She smiled when she saw that it was delicately nibbling on some lettuce, only to dart back into its towel burrow when it spotted her. At least it was feeling well enough to act more like a wild animal. That was a relief.

"I know I'm not keeping you as a pet," she said to the rabbit, "but calling you 'the rabbit' is awkward. You need a good name. I also have no idea if you're a boy or a girl." She rubbed her chin, thinking.

The rabbit wiggled its nose, and right in front of Thea, it grabbed the edge of the last bit of lettuce and pulled it into its burrow. That made her laugh.

"I'm calling you Sneaky," she declared as she tore up some more lettuce and placed it in the box. "Sneaky the rabbit, who steals lettuce right from under your nose if you aren't careful. I'm also going to think of you as a boy, which I'm sure matters greatly to you."

Sneaky just munched on his lettuce, not the least bit perturbed by his new name or supposed gender.

Thea's phone rang, and she grimaced when she saw that Mittens was calling. He'd been texting her nonstop for days, and she'd only replied a few times. The fact that he was calling a second time today? Not good.

"Are you dead?" were Mittens's first words when she finally answered.

"Considering I just answered my phone, no."

"Then why are you ignoring me?"

That was a good question, to which she had no answer. *Because I don't know if I want to go through with getting dirt on Anthony. Because he kissed me like no other man has ever kissed me. Because I'm losing my damn mind.*

"I've been busy," she hedged.

"Busy. When you're stuck in a cabin in the middle of nowhere. I'm hoping you got some good intel on Bertram if you've been so *busy*."

Thea had done some research on Anthony's ex-wife, Elise Edgerton, who was now remarried and called Elise Weaver. She had looked at photos of the couple and read articles from when they'd gotten divorced. No one had known why they'd suddenly split. One day they were photographed at dinner, looking as cozy as ever. The next, Anthony had filed for divorce, citing irreconcilable differences.

Thea was sure that he'd gotten Elise to sign an ironclad nondisclosure agreement along with the settlement Elise must've received. None of that, however, was a part of the public record.

Thea wondered what could've happened between them. Had someone cheated? Or had Elise wanted to end things because she'd fallen out of love with Anthony? Or vice versa?

"I saw the *Society* article they did on the company," said Mittens. "I'm sure he was pissed about that. Did you see it? It was not flattering at all." Mittens sounded gleeful.

Thea pulled up the article in question and scanned it. She grimaced as she read it. No, it wasn't flattering in the least.

"No wonder he's been such an asshole lately," she said, sighing. "He's like a baited bear most days."

"Which proves our point. He's an asshole, just like you said. Think of the rabbits, Thea. The rats, the dogs. All the animals that suffer for his wallet." With each word, Mittens's voice rose. "We're doing something important, something that will make a difference. Although why I'm the one saying this when it was your idea, I don't know."

Thea glanced over at Sneaky, her heart pinching in dismay. The thought of doing experiments on Sneaky was heartbreaking. He might just be a rabbit, but he was also a living, breathing creature that had a mind of its own. Shouldn't that be respected and cherished, when the world always seemed such an unfeeling place?

Thea replied, "No, I know. I'm trying to find some information, but he doesn't leave his room much. The rain only just stopped, although it's so muddy it's not great for wandering around outside, so he's in the cabin most of the time." She decided not to mention the bit about finding that photo of him and Elise. It wasn't like it revealed anything new, anyway—right?

"Don't give up. You'll find something. I believe in you." Mittens let out a sigh. "When are you coming back? I know you said two weeks, but it's been *so* boring here. I need my drinking buddy back."

"Just another week, hopefully. Although with the bridge out, it could be longer."

Mittens groaned. "Please don't tell me that. I'll get a helicopter to come save you. Or a jet. A hot-air balloon? Whatever. But not until you get something on this guy. Do it for the bunnies, Thea. Do it for them."

After the call ended, Thea sat on her bed, thinking. She felt like she was being torn in two. It was easy to think of Anthony as a heartless monster. You didn't have to worry about hurting a monster's feelings, because they *had* no feelings.

But the more she got to know Anthony, the more she felt that he wasn't the monster she'd thought he was. He was still an ass, and he still rankled her most of the time. His company was still evil.

But she also knew that most situations—and people— weren't drawn in shades of black and white. Life loved to be shades of gray, and Thea found herself falling into a gray area that she had no idea how to navigate.

She also knew that she was a total hypocrite. She'd been too much of a coward to tell Anthony who she really was. At first, it was solely out of self-preservation. Why reveal her identity to him when they were stuck together, and he could make her life hell as a result?

Now, though, she hated herself for lying to him. He thought she was someone she wasn't. She didn't regret being a part of that campaign, yet at the same time, she couldn't find the courage to speak the truth.

She needed to stop this—whatever *this* was—before it went too far. The kiss had been a sign that she was getting in way too deep already. If she just avoided Anthony entirely and created a firm boundary, she could get out of here without destroying herself in the process.

"No more kissing," Thea muttered to herself as she lay down. "No more touching. No more getting to know him. Don't be an idiot, Thea. You're better than this."

She kept reciting that vow over and over as she fell asleep, only to have that kiss haunt her dreams.

Anthony didn't see Thea the next morning. He assumed she was sleeping in, although she normally ate breakfast pretty early. He scowled at her door, then scowled at himself for acting like some hormonal teenage boy.

They'd kissed last night. So what? He'd kissed plenty of women. Since his divorce, he'd had a string of lovers, the relationships never lasting beyond a few weeks, if the woman was lucky. The women had all known they were temporary, and they'd been fine with it. When Anthony needed that itch scratched, he got it done. Just like he did everything else in his life.

Since he'd first met Elise, he'd never been turned down by any woman he wanted. Why would he be? He was rich and handsome and knew how to make a woman scream his name in bed. Gossip like that spread quickly, and he'd used it to his advantage.

So why did it bother him so much that Thea had essentially rejected him after that kiss? Especially since she'd seemed so enthusiastic at first? It made no sense whatsoever.

He glowered at nothing as he headed outside. He needed some air. The cabin reminded him of Thea—the smells, the sounds, the stupid tofu wraps she made for lunch. The bag of quinoa on the counter had basically sat there, judging him, when he'd gone into the kitchen. Like it knew he had upset its mistress. The thought had been so ridiculous that Anthony had taken the bag and shoved into a cabinet, out of sight.

Anthony reminded himself of what had happened the last time he'd let a woman overtake his senses. He'd become obsessed with Elise, and although he'd never admit it, he'd worked himself to the bone to prove to her that he was worthy of her. And then he'd made her his.

He'd thought their marriage had been happy at the time. He had been away a lot because of his business, taking flights all around the world, from Beijing to Montreal to London. Sometimes Elise had joined him; most times she'd preferred to stay in Seattle. She'd had her own friends to keep her company while he was gone.

Everything had changed when Anthony had hired Ryan Weaver. Ryan, who had been his roommate in college. Who'd been Anthony's friend far longer than Elise had been his wife. Ryan, who'd helped take Bertram, Sons, and Co. to the next level while also stealing Elise from him.

Anthony kicked at a rock that tumbled down the hill toward the broken bridge. He imagined it was Ryan's face. The backstabbing, scheming bastard. He'd soon begun to hate that Anthony was CEO, and he'd been second best. So he'd gotten one up on Anthony and had seduced Elise right under his nose. Although that implied Elise had had no choice in the matter—she'd made her bed when she had betrayed Anthony in the worst possible way.

The evening he'd discovered their betrayal, Anthony had come home after spending ten days in China. He'd been jet-lagged, hungry, and desperately in need of a shower.

It was the middle of the night, and since Elise was already asleep, Anthony grabbed a quick bite from the kitchen and went upstairs. As he walked to their bedroom, Anthony heard a thump. He waited, listening, wondering if Elise was awake for some reason. Considering it was close to three a.m., he couldn't imagine why she'd be awake so late on a Wednesday.

He heard another thump, then a giggle. He was jet-lagged enough not to realize what it was right away.

Pushing the master bedroom door open, he heard someone gasp, and then a rustling. He flipped on the light.

And there, both naked as the day they were born, were his wife and his best friend. Anthony didn't need any more explanation than that.

Rage filled him. Without a second thought, he dragged Ryan from the bed and punched him in the gut. Elise screamed, blubbering excuses. Ryan, for his part, didn't put up a fight. He just held up his hands and tried his best to explain.

But what was there to explain? Anthony gave Ryan a bloody nose and another kick in the ribs before hissing, "You piece of shit. I trusted you."

It was only Elise grabbing onto his arm that stopped him from killing Ryan.

Wiping the sweat from his upper lip, Anthony growled, "Get out. Before I take a gun and blow your brains out."

Ryan scooped up his clothes, but seeing Anthony's expression, he didn't even get dressed. He scurried out of there, tail between his legs, his bare white ass winking in the dim light.

Elise tried to reason with him. But he just handed her her clothes and said, "This is over."

She was sobbing, saying that she'd made a mistake, it hadn't meant anything. Anthony didn't care.

The next day, he filed for divorce. Considering the grounds he had against Elise, she didn't put up much of a fight. Anthony had gotten all parties to sign an NDA. He'd refused to let this story get leaked to the press. The last thing he needed was some scandal involving his former VP and his ex-wife. Not only would it be humiliating, but it could seriously jeopardize his already tenuous position as CEO. If the board thought he couldn't keep a hold of his own employees or his wife, they could side with Bruce and oust him from the company he'd built himself.

But Ryan had only agreed to keep his mouth shut if he got hush money along with company stock. Despite how much he'd hated doing it, Anthony had agreed. Everything had been fine until Elise had started squawking about needing more money.

The thought of losing his company was worse than losing Elise. He could move on from heartbreak. He couldn't move on from what had basically become his heart, mind, and soul since its inception when he'd just been a young undergraduate at the University of Washington.

He ended up down at the creek, watching the water without really seeing it.

More importantly, he needed to get this attraction for Thea under control. She would only be a distraction. She wasn't the type of person who would bring anything to the empire he was building. She'd try to get him to give all his money to charities for orphaned rabbits, knowing her.

His lips quirked, thinking of that rabbit in its box up at the cabin. And then he frowned. That rabbit represented only weakness, a weakness he'd given in to and shouldn't have.

So he forced himself to think of Elise, of how she'd betrayed him, of how he had to hold on to this company no matter the cost, and it gave him the strength to return to the cabin and act like Thea didn't even exist.

CHAPTER NINE

Thea finished chopping an onion and was about to throw it into a bowl when the lights flickered. Then she heard a huge popping sound before the entire cabin was plunged into darkness.

Turning off the burner behind her, she waited a few more minutes, hoping the power would come back on. The darkness persisted. Sighing, she turned on her phone's flashlight, swearing under her breath when she saw that her battery was low.

"Did you hear that?" called Anthony from the living room. He came into the kitchen, the light of his flashlight brighter than Thea's phone.

"Yeah, I heard it." Thea sighed her displeasure. Although the rain had stopped, a windstorm had blown in, and apparently it had done something to make the power go off.

"I'm going to go check what it was. It's probably the generator," said Anthony.

Thea frowned at Anthony's retreating back. Since when did some pampered billionaire know how to fix a generator?

Morbidly curious, she put on her boots and followed him outside.

"You don't have to come outside with me," he said as he opened the shed some yards from the cabin.

"I can hold the flashlight for you." She flashed him a wide smile.

He grunted, handing her the flashlight before getting a toolbox down from a nearby shelf. Thea stopped at the same shelf, over which a large, taxidermied fish hung on the wall. She had no idea why anyone would preserve a fish like that. Then again, she didn't understand why anyone would preserve a deer head, either. She shuddered.

"What's the point?" she asked, not expecting a response.

Anthony cocked an eyebrow. "What? Of a toolbox?"

She rolled her eyes. "No, the fish on the wall. If you're going to take the time to catch a fish, why not eat it?"

"I thought you were against eating animals."

"I am, but it seems more of a waste to stick it on your wall."

Anthony shrugged. "I guess it's to remember the hard work that went into catching it."

Thea grunted.

"Why don't you eat meat?" he asked suddenly.

She waited for him to mock her, but when he just waited for her response, she said, "I wasn't always vegan, but when I did more research into how animals suffer for our food, I made a change. I feel a lot healthier for it, and nothing has to die to feed me."

"Plants had to die."

"Like I've never heard that one before." She rolled her eyes. "Plants can't feel. And don't tell me that you can't get protein as a vegan, because there are lots of plant-based proteins you can eat."

His lips twitched. "I wasn't going to say that at all."

The moment settled, and Thea couldn't help but remember how he'd kissed her only a day prior. Ever since then, he'd barely said two words to her, and to her annoyance, it had stung. She'd also avoided him, but he'd been the one to kiss her in the first place. You didn't get to kiss a woman like that and then act like she was nothing more than a piece of furniture.

As his gaze heated, Thea felt goose bumps rise on her skin. Rubbing her arms, she muttered, "It's cold."

At that reminder, the moment shattered. Anthony's expression closed, and just like that, a wall was once again between them.

Thea wished she wasn't so intrigued by him to want to climb over that wall to discover who the real Anthony Bertram was.

Anthony kneeled down in front of the generator and switched something off before opening the front panel. Thea stood next to him, holding the flashlight so he could see what he was doing.

She couldn't stop herself from drinking in the strength of his shoulders, or the way his hair was a bit too long and curled near the neck of his shirt. He had a mole on the right side of the throat. She had the sudden, insane urge to lick him right there.

She bit her lip. When the flashlight wavered, Anthony glanced up at her. She fought a blush. "Sorry," she muttered.

He returned to his work, allowing her to continue looking at him without him realizing it. She'd thought he was handsome since she'd seen that first photo of him online, and he was only more handsome in person. He was also more commanding, and taller, and—

Thea shook herself. *Stop fantasizing. Even if this went somewhere, do you think he'd stick around after he found out what you did to him?*

That thought alone made her shoulders slump. Then she chastised herself for caring.

Hating the silence, she cleared her throat. "Where did you learn how to repair generators?" she finally asked, realizing she was genuinely curious. It didn't seem like something a guy like him would know about.

"Believe it or not, my family lived in the middle of nowhere when I was a kid." He inspected what looked like some kind of filter. "Our house was run on a generator. My dad taught me how to fix them."

She didn't know why she was shocked. Maybe it was because imagining Anthony as a kid was weird enough, let alone a kid living in the middle of nowhere. It sounded so *normal.*

"Was it just you? No brothers or sisters?"

"I had a younger sister, but she passed away when she was only two. I was four, so I barely remember her." At Thea's questioning look, he added, "It was a brain tumor. One of those you can't do anything about, basically."

"Jesus, I'm so sorry. That's awful."

Anthony shrugged. "Like I said, I barely remember her."

"That doesn't make it any less a tragedy."

He paused. Then: "I guess you're right."

As if she didn't want to consider that his words made him seem more human, she continued to chatter to fill the silence.

"I couldn't imagine losing any of my siblings. I have four. Two brothers and a sister."

Anthony grunted. "That sounds loud."

She laughed. "Pretty much. We were a crazy bunch. Still are."

She thought of her siblings when they were kids, how they'd stuck together when their parents had started falling apart. Their mother, Beatrice, had killed herself, and their father Edward had been a mean, angry man. No one had mourned when he'd passed just a few years ago.

"Do you see your parents ever?" Thea asked.

"My dad passed five years ago. My mom lives in London with her new husband."

Thea's heart pinched. So he was alone, especially now that he was divorced. Was that why he had so many walls up? She wished she didn't care so much. She should follow Mittens's advice and only use this information to take down his company. But the thought of betraying his trust like that made her stomach turn.

"My parents are both dead," she offered.

He paused. "I'm sorry," he said gruffly.

"No one was sad when my dad went. My mom…" She sighed. "Anyway, I have my siblings, and my new sisters-in-law. And my niece. I think that's more than enough family."

"I wouldn't know." He sounded irritated now.

Thea fought against hurt, but she couldn't help but wonder if talk of family was painful for him. Although if she ever said as much, he'd probably bite her head off.

Anthony rose and went to the other side of the generator. He pulled to move it away from the wall before he swore, long and low.

"What? Did you figure out what's wrong?" said Thea.

"Look." He pointed, and she shined the flashlight in that direction. A leak had apparently sprung near the floor and the wall, and the bottom of the generator was soaking wet.

"God only knows how much water has gotten inside it. I'm surprised it stayed on as long as it did," he said.

"So, what does that mean? Is it broken?"

He shook his head. "But we can't turn it on without seriously damaging it until we let it dry out. Even then, some of the parts inside might be too damaged to be reused." He looked around, going to a nearby shelf. "Looks like there's a new hose I can install, but even then, the generator has to dry out."

"How long will that take?"

"I don't know. A day or two, maybe longer." Anthony pulled out his phone, only to swear again. "Dammit, I have no service. What about you?"

Thea pulled out her phone, too. "Me either. It must be from the wind."

Outside, the wind howled, as if agreeing with Thea's assessment.

"Help me pull the generator out. We'll move it to a dry spot and hope for the best," said Anthony.

She helped him move the generator and set it on a shelf to dry. After they'd set it down, her shirt was wet from all the water that had gotten caught inside the generator. Even Thea, who knew nothing about machines, knew that that much water inside a machine wasn't good.

It was only when she caught Anthony's gaze that she realized that she'd very stupidly worn a light-colored shirt that was currently see-through from all the water that had soaked through it. Anthony's jaw was tight, his eyes blazing. Thea felt her nipples harden, which only made him look more hostile. A fire burned in her belly.

And then he turned away. Disappointed, she sighed to herself. It was better this way. She knew that.

~

ANTHONY GATHERED as much firewood he could, but the roof that was supposed to keep the firewood dry had sprung a leak. *Of course*, he thought acidly. Some of the firewood was still usable, but much of it was too wet and would have to dry out like the generator.

Thea was sitting in the living room when he came inside. To his disappointment, she'd changed out of her wet t-shirt into something dry.

He'd been able to see almost everything through that wet shirt: her nipples, the shape of her breasts, the indentation of her belly button. It had taken all of his self-control not to haul her to him and kiss her again.

He let out an annoyed breath as he began to arrange the wood in the fireplace. Anthony also didn't know why he'd told her about his childhood or his parents. It wasn't that he was ashamed of where he'd come from, but he wasn't much for talking about his childhood. Even Elise hadn't met his mother, who hadn't been in the States for many years since remarrying.

"I'm going to call Ted," he said as he ripped up old newspapers for kindling. "This is absolutely ridiculous. I didn't sign up for Little House on the Fucking Prairie."

Thea snorted. "I can't imagine you churning butter."

He glanced over his shoulder. "I wouldn't be the one churning the butter. That's for the women."

"Oh, please. Real men can churn butter." Her expression sobering, she said, "Thank you for doing all this. I'm glad you knew what to do, because God knows I don't have any wilderness skills."

He turned back to the fireplace. Her thanking him—again—only made him want to tell her never to say those words. He wasn't doing this for her. He was doing it for himself, just like he did everything else. He never did anything without a motive.

But now that he'd gone down memory lane, he couldn't help but think how he'd come to this point. After his little sister had died, it was like his parents had decided that she hadn't existed. Anthony hadn't thought of Gretchen in ages. He'd been so young that her loss hadn't registered in his mind. Yet now, the bits of memories he had of her saddened him. He wondered how his parents had coped with losing a child. Or had they coped at all?

Irritated with his morose thoughts, he picked up the poker by the wrong end, where it had already been heated by the fire. His hand burning, he dropped it with a colorful string of curses.

"Are you okay?" Thea rushed to him. "What happened?"

He gritted his teeth. "Nothing. It's fine." But his palm was on fire, and when he opened his hand, he hissed. God, he was an idiot. He'd gotten so distracted that he'd picked up a hot poker.

"You're not fine. Did you burn yourself?" Thea clasped his wrist and held his hand to the fire to get a better look. She clucked her tongue. "Sit down. I'll be right back."

Anthony wanted to protest, as he didn't like to be fussed over, but Thea just pointed at the couch. He found himself obeying. She soon returned with a bowl of water and a rag that she dipped in the water.

"Most people think you should put ice on a burn, but actually you should put just cool water on it. When I was a kid, my younger sister Lucy burned her finger on the stove and I remembered that we learned that tip in school. Handy, right?"

She took his burned hand and gently wrapped the wet cloth around it. He winced at the contact, but the wet cloth lessened the severity of the pain in a few moments.

They sat there in silence. The burn on his palm faded away as he focused on the feeling of Thea's hand that still clasped his.

He didn't need her to hold the cloth on his palm. He could do it himself. But he didn't want to tell her to stop.

The firelight flickered across her face. In profile, she was beautiful. He told himself that her nose was too long, her chin too pointed, to be considered beautiful. He didn't understand the point of having a septum piercing like that, through the middle of her nose like a bullring. Her hair was too short, too bleached; her nails were painted some garish orange that was chipping. Her tattoos were overly bright and colorful, covering her entire arm like a shirtsleeve.

But she smelled so good, and when she smiled, it was like the clouds parted and the sun finally shone through. God, he wanted her. He wanted to lick and taste every inch of her pale skin. He wanted to hear her moan his name when he was inside her.

Yet he knew that sleeping with her would be a terrible

idea. Thea wasn't the type of woman who wanted a one-night stand. She would want everything—the commitment, the ring, the white picket fence. The declarations of love. Despite her appearance, she was as conventional as apple pie. And Anthony didn't like apple pie.

As if sensing where his thoughts were going, Thea let go of his hand and moved further away from him on the couch.

"I need to check on Sneaky," she said, getting up. "Is your hand feeling better?"

"Who's Sneaky?"

"The rabbit." At his confused expression, she shrugged. "He was sneaky about eating his food. And I thought it was cute."

She went upstairs, leaving Anthony to ponder that response. Of course she'd named the rabbit. Knowing her, she'd keep it as a pet and carry it around in her purse.

He blew out a breath. Pulling the wet cloth from his hand, he flexed his fingers. Although the burn still stung, it wasn't as bad as it could have been.

Thea returned downstairs carrying a cardboard box. "What are you doing?" she said. "You need to keep that cloth on there." She set the box on the coffee table.

"You brought the rabbit?" he asked, peering down into it.

"It's cold upstairs. Anyway, I need to feed him. I'm going to get something to eat, too. Want anything?"

It was ridiculous, but the question sounded so wifely that it made him feel things he didn't want to feel.

Roughly, he said, "I don't eat rabbit food."

A flash of hurt crossed Thea's face, but she masked it well. Anthony refused to feel guilty.

He couldn't let her get too close.

CHAPTER TEN

Thea was tempted to leave Anthony to his gloomy thoughts, but she didn't want to freeze upstairs. Granted, it wasn't *that* cold, but it was the principle of the thing.

She sat down on the couch next to him with two plates of food: one for her, and one for Sneaky. She tore up some of the lettuce and placed it inside the box. She smiled when Sneaky immediately began eating. Soon, she'd have to figure out a way to let him get some exercise. She'd tried to let him hop around her room earlier, but he'd hidden in a corner the entire time.

Thea then bit into a carrot stick of her own, loudly crunching it. Anthony raised a sardonic eyebrow, but she just smiled widely.

"You said you have four siblings?" said Anthony apropos of nothing.

It was her turn to raise an eyebrow. *Why did he suddenly care?* She bit into another carrot. "Yeah. Why?"

He shrugged. "I could tell. You acted like an older sister."

She wanted to snort. She sure as hell hadn't been thinking about Anthony like an *older sister.* Wouldn't her siblings just laugh at her now if they could see her?

"I had to help take care of my siblings when we were young," she said with a shrug. "I guess bossing people around is just a part of me now."

Anthony didn't ask her anything else. Thea refused to let the silence draw out. If he wanted to know about her siblings, then why not tell him? He could sit and listen to her prattle on for hours. The thought amused her enough for her to continue talking.

She told him about how her family had been middle class until their father, Edward, had lost his job, and then things had gone downhill. The family had struggled to put food on the table. It hadn't helped that their mother, Beatrice, had been suffering from undiagnosed mental illness—most likely bipolar disorder, Thea had discovered later—and Edward had taken out his anger and frustration on Beatrice.

To anyone else, telling this man about her childhood and her family might've seemed strange. But Thea had this ridiculous urge to connect with him, to draw out that vulnerable, caring side of him that she'd seen flashes of. She knew it existed. She'd seen it when he'd saved Sneaky. So why did he usually hide it? If she made herself vulnerable, maybe he would drop his guard, too.

"When my mom died, I had to take on a lot of responsibilities," she explained. "My younger siblings needed a mom. I tried my best to be one."

It hadn't been that simple, of course. What twelve-year-old knew how to take care of her traumatized siblings? Thea had been little more than a child herself. At least she'd had her older brother Trent to lean on. The two of them had managed well enough together, with their father doing little more than paying for the leaky roof over their heads and some meals. After Beatrice had died, it had been like Edward had just given up entirely.

"I wanted to leave for ages, but I couldn't leave my siblings. I did move out, though, but I still helped take care of Ash, Phin and Lucy until they were old enough to fend for themselves."

Anthony hadn't said anything in a while. He was gazing at seemingly nothing, and Thea wondered if he'd been listening at all.

"You're not angry about any of that?" he finally asked. He looked her in the face now as he spoke. "You didn't hate your parents for taking away your childhood? Or resent your siblings for making you stay?"

"Maybe when I was younger, I did, but I guess I don't hold on to anger like that. It wasn't my siblings' fault, either. And I've seen how my parents hurt them. I'm not saying the hurt isn't still there." She shrugged, because she didn't know if she could explain it.

She'd never hated her parents. She'd hated the circumstances. She'd hated that no one outside of the family had tried to help. She'd wished that things could've been different. But what did hate and anger do? Would they somehow take away what had happened? She'd soon learned that holding onto anger didn't help anyone.

"I forgave my parents a long time ago," said Thea softly.

Anthony looked incredulous. "Why? They didn't deserve that."

His voice was hard, his expression even harder. She didn't

fully understand why he was so intent on her answer. She had a distinct feeling this had nothing to do with her parents at all.

"It wasn't about them deserving it," she said slowly, "but about letting myself keep living. Forgiveness isn't for the perpetrator—not really. It's for you. It's freeing. That's all. I couldn't let the cycle continue with me, even though it would've been easier, I guess."

Anthony looked at her like he'd never heard anyone say something so crazy. But Thea knew she wasn't crazy. She'd seen how anger had hurt Trent, how it had kept Ash walled away from the world.

Needing to break the tension, Thea muttered, "It's still really dark in here." She went into the kitchen and opened one of the cabinets, frowning when she found her bag of quinoa amongst a bunch of cups and plates. She finally found a drawer with tea candles. Placing a few on a plate, she brought them into the living room and lit them.

But lighting candles had been a mistake, because it only made the entire scene feel cozier. More intimate. More romantic. Thea wiped her sweaty palms on her jeans, feeling stupid for being so self-conscious.

Anthony, for his part, seemed far away.

"When do you think the power will turn back on?" ventured Thea.

Anthony didn't reply. She repeated the question, and he finally looked at her, as if he were surprised she was still sitting there.

"Um, I don't know. I called Ted, but the call was dropped. Who knows, with this wind?" Anthony leaned back onto the couch, his arms crossed, before asking, "How did you do it?"

"Do what?"

"Forgive your parents."

She wasn't sure how to explain. "I mean, there isn't like a checklist," she joked. At his grim stare, she said more seriously, "It was just a mental decision, but I also went to my parents' graves, too, to tell them. Like I said, it was for me, not them."

"And that's it? You just forget everything happened?"

"No, you don't forget. Do you ever forget? No, you just…" She chewed on her lower lip, thinking. "You move past it. Sorry, I'm not great at explaining. My last boyfriend always said that I was too forgiving. That's probably why I dumped him," she added wryly.

Anthony's expression lightened somewhat. "Probably." Then: "What about your latest boyfriend?"

His tone seemed nonchalant. She couldn't read him at all. "I don't have a latest boyfriend," she whispered. She took a deep breath. "What about you?"

"What about me?"

"Are you married, have a girlfriend…?"

"No. Considering we kissed last night, if either of us had said yes, it would be rather awkward."

Thea shivered at the memory. "Of course. Sorry. I wasn't thinking."

Anthony continued, "No, I'm not married. In fact, I've been single for two years since my divorce. It might have soured my outlook on marriage in general." His voice was wry, although Thea could detect an underlying bitterness, too.

She thought of the photo she'd found in his briefcase, the articles online about his divorce. But the articles hadn't mentioned why they'd divorced, and they certainly hadn't taken into account the hurt that would result from a breakup that had clearly once been a love match based on that photo.

Jealousy nipped at her, that that woman had gotten to see a side of Anthony Thea would never get to see. What had he been like as a husband? she wondered. Had he been attentive? Sweet? Or had he treated it like any other business deal? Her curiosity almost overwhelmed her.

Right then, their gazes collided, then held, the tension in the room increasing until Thea struggled to take a deep breath. She couldn't help but stare at his mouth: his lips were plush, but his jaw was hard. She remembered how he'd kissed her, how strong his arms had been around her. Her skin prickled, goose bumps dotting her arms. When she licked her lips, his forehead creased, his nostrils flaring.

Despite her best intentions and despite every thought in her head telling her it was a bad idea, Thea wanted Anthony to kiss her again. She wanted *him*—so much. She practically ached with the need spiraling tighter inside her.

Her knee brushed Anthony's as she moved closer to him, like an invisible string pulled her along. He didn't tell her to stop. Emboldened, she touched his knee, skimming her fingers upward, her intention crystal clear.

"You're playing with fire," he said hoarsely.

She smiled. "Is that a warning? Or a promise?"

"Both."

Then she was in his arms as he kissed her. His mouth was hot, devouring. She clung to him, letting herself get swept away by sheer sensation. Her entire body burned. The stubble on his chin and cheeks scraped at her tender skin, but it only heightened the intensity of his kiss.

Anthony Bertram kissed like a fiend. There was no other way to describe it. Where Thea's previous lovers had been almost tentative, Anthony was dominating. He thrust his tongue into her mouth, tipping her head back. Thea could only surrender. She'd never been the type to be passive, but in this instance, she could only bend to his will.

But her passivity could only last so long. She broke the kiss. At his growl, she pressed a finger to his mouth and climbed onto his lap. Now they were face-to-face, and she could touch him like she'd wanted to do since the first moment she'd seen him.

Thea began to unbutton his shirt. He hitched in a breath, watching her intently. Unveiling his chest covered in dark hair, she leaned forward and pressed a kiss right over his heart.

ANTHONY BIT BACK A GROAN. Thea's clever fingers continued to unbutton his shirt, skimming across his skin with a touch like a butterfly's. His cock pressed against the zipper of his jeans, almost painfully hard, and he'd only kissed her. She shot him an impish smile that boded ill for him.

He should push her away. And then he should go upstairs and lock his door for good measure. He should tell her this was a beyond stupid idea that would only get her hurt and him distracted. He needed to focus on his company. He needed to avoid entanglements with women who would want commitment. He needed to—

Thea kissed him over his heart, and his breath caught in his throat. It was such a small gesture, but it was like being pushed into a river. Swept away in the current, he could only kiss her again, tasting lemons with every brush of his lips against hers.

He pushed her shirt up until he could splay his hand on

her lower back. Her skin was silky soft, and when he traced the bumps of her vertebrae, she shivered.

She barely weighed anything, sitting on his lap, but her warmth and strength were unmistakable in every inch of her body. When he traced a figure-eight in the middle of her back, right below her bra, she wiggled, her crotch rubbing against his.

He hissed, holding her still. "This is going to be over before we've started," he muttered, glaring at her.

She dimpled, and God Almighty, it only made him harder. She tried wiggling again, and he wrapped his arm harder around her.

"Bad girls get punished," he whispered in her ear, "and if you keep doing that, you'll be next on the list."

"Oh, I'm very, very scared." Thea nipped at his shoulder.

"Don't bite, brat." Anthony moved his hand to cup one of her breasts, and she let out a deep sigh of satisfaction when he thumbed her nipple through her bra. He desperately wanted to see her naked, drink in every inch of her, but he was trying to restrain himself. Because if he had her in his bed once, he wouldn't stop himself from taking her again and again until they finally went their separate ways.

He played with her for a while, just touching, learning the hills and valleys of her. She did the same, delving beneath the edges of his shirt. She flicked one of his nipples with her nail. He growled before lifting her shirt over her head and tossing it away.

Her breasts were small but well-formed, and her nipples were hard little peaks through the sheer lace of her bra. He pushed her bra straps down her arms, and finally, her breasts were free and bare. He drank in the gorgeous sight: her nipples were puffy, a dark rose color, and he could see blue veins below her creamy skin.

Thea ran her fingers through his hair, scratching at his scalp. "Anthony…" she whispered.

He licked one breast, tonguing a nipple before he sucked it into his mouth. Thea moaned, long and low, only giving him more of a reason to continue. He laved each breast until she was gasping and shivering. He wondered if he could make her come just by sucking on her breasts.

But he needed more. Cupping her sex through her jeans, he began to rub her, the heat of her almost burning his palm. Thea sucked in a breath before she began to undulate with him. When he found the right spot, he pressed harder. Thea leaned down and bit his shoulder again as she rocked with him.

"Are you going to come for me?" he growled. He tugged her head up so he could see into her eyes. "Tell me, Thea. Are you?"

Her eyes were glassy, her cheeks flushed. "Yes, yes—"

Her back arched. Her eyes rolled back inside her head. And then she bit down on her lip hard as her orgasm made her body shake. It was the most erotic thing he'd ever seen in his life. Not wanting this to end already, Anthony drew out her release until she finally collapsed against his chest.

They stayed like that for a long moment. Anthony stroked her back, his chin on the crown of her head. Thea's breathing slowed before she finally sat up again.

Her hands reached for his fly, but he pushed her away. "Not tonight."

She frowned. "But—"

"You should go upstairs." At his brusque tone, she flinched. He said more gently, "Go."

She hesitated, like she wanted to demand answers. He looked away from her.

Finally, she got up, grabbing her shirt and Sneaky in his box before heading upstairs.

Anthony stayed in the living room for a while, taking deep breaths, trying to order his thoughts. He was still hard, and it had taken everything in him not to let Thea touch him, too. But he knew if anyone was playing with fire, it was him.

He'd already given in to too much temptation. Any further and he wouldn't return.

CHAPTER ELEVEN

Thea couldn't sleep all night. She tossed and turned until she finally gave up around five in the morning. Going downstairs, she made coffee, bringing Sneaky along with her.

Setting up a pen of sorts with various furniture while lining the floor with towels, she let Sneaky begin to explore his new digs. At first he stayed in the corner, but eventually he found the courage to venture further out. It helped that Thea had placed a nice pile of lettuce and carrots for him to munch on in the middle of the pen. Sneaky was still favoring his right leg, though. Once they were able to get out of this cabin, she'd take him to a vet to be looked at.

She blew out a breath as she sat down on the oversized leather chair near the remains of the fire from the night before. The candles she'd lit had burned down to puddles of wax. She shivered, wishing she knew how to start a fire. It couldn't be that difficult, right? She'd watched Anthony do it last night.

Thea lined the fireplace with newspaper and added fresh wood. To her delight, the fire started without an issue. But it didn't take long for it to burn out. She tried again and had the same result.

Irritated, she collapsed back onto her chair and stewed. Her thoughts inevitably strayed to Anthony, and how he'd kissed her last night. How he'd done more than kiss her. She closed her eyes, feeling his hands on her back, remembering the way he'd groaned her name. How he'd kissed her, how he'd brought her to her release.

And how he'd basically sent her to her room without one look back. She'd thought he'd wanted her as much as she'd wanted him, but she'd been wrong. It was like the light had gone out of his eyes. Or worse, he'd realized he'd made a mistake.

Thea winced. She didn't want to be someone's mistake. And how dare Anthony treat her like that, as if she had the plague? Her nails bit into her palm, so hard that they left crescents in her skin. He'd wanted her in the beginning—she knew when a man wanted her. So what had changed between the ravenous kisses and the cold parting?

Irritated, she got up to stoke the fire a third time, but when the fire burned out within minutes, she almost tossed the poker across the room. She then imagined using it to hit Anthony in the back of the head, and she felt a little better.

He's an asshole, Thea reminded herself. *He doesn't care about anyone but himself. You already knew that.*

If he thought of her as a mistake, he must think she was beneath him. She was nobody, especially compared to his ex-wife: she wasn't some rich, beautiful socialite. Thea was just a struggling artist from a messed-up family. She winced, thinking of how she'd told him about her family.

Oh God, what if he was disgusted with her family history?

What if he thought she could be crazy like her mother? Trembling with anger, she tried to steady her breathing and keep her thoughts from running every which way. Getting worked up without knowing for certain wouldn't help her.

Mittens texted her later that morning, nothing in the message but a single link. Opening the website, Thea's eyes slowly widened more and more as she read through the article Mittens had texted her.

By the end of the article, she was fuming. *Bertram, Sons, and Co. dedicates itself to providing the best customer experience*, was the headline that meant essentially nothing. The article was all praise, including testimonials from customers. But it was the tiny paragraph near the end that made Thea want to set Anthony's bed on fire—with him in it.

In order to provide our customers in all countries with our products, animal testing is an unfortunate necessity. We continue to look for other options, however. We thank everyone for their feedback on this divisive issue.

Thea knew very well that they didn't have to test on animals at all. Many companies avoided that. She could name a dozen that she used herself that were cruelty-free. She imagined Sneaky as one of those unfortunate animals who was fed poisons or burned with chemicals before getting tossed out like trash.

Her anger only spiked higher when Mittens texted, *In case you needed to be reminded why he's an asshole.*

Yes, she'd needed the reminder. Although guilt wanted to win in regard to Anthony, her disgust eclipsed it. A man who didn't care about innocent animals wasn't capable of caring for her. She'd needed to remember that he was heartless and not worthy of her empathy.

I think being stuck with him has gone to my head, she texted back with a sobbing emoji. *I need to get out of here!*

Obviously. And I need you back because we're putting together another campaign. If Bertram and his people are going to double down on this shit, then we will, too.

Thea swallowed against the lump in her throat before replying, *Count me in.*

She returned upstairs and spent the morning drawing before her stomach began to rumble. Wandering downstairs, she found Anthony in the living room. And to her immense dismay, he was feeding Sneaky bites of carrots. He smiled when the rabbit took the last nub of a carrot from him, a smile that went straight through Thea's heart and made her ovaries explode.

How could a man who ran a company like his be like this in person? She couldn't make it out at all. She couldn't help but wonder if he even cared about the animals that were being tested on. Would he be this kind to *them?* She had a feeling she already knew the answer.

"I thought you didn't like animals," she said. Her anger from earlier returned within moments.

He stood up, cocking an eyebrow. "So much that I helped you save one from certain death?" he said dryly.

"You only did that so I wouldn't break my neck. You said so yourself."

Thea knew she sounded combative, but she was in a combative mood. She was tired of seeing this kind side of Anthony. She needed to be reminded of the asshole that lurked beneath.

"True." He glanced back at Sneaky. "He is cute, I have to admit."

"He's a rabbit. They're all cute."

"Look, Thea, if you're upset about last night—"

She shook her head. "Last night doesn't matter. I've already forgotten it." *Liar.* "I just want to know one thing: why are you so kind to Sneaky when your company tests on animals, and continues to do so even when it's bad PR?"

She probably could have asked less boldly, but she didn't care if she offended him.

Anthony's expression shuddered, and Thea could practically see him put on his cold CEO mask. Stepping toward her, he said quietly, "What is this about, Thea?"

"Exactly what I just said. I don't get you at all. One second you're torturing animals for profit. The next you're saving a rabbit from starving or drowning."

"It's complicated."

"Then explain it to me."

"You seem very intent on this. Why?"

At the spark in his eyes, she looked away, her throat dry. *Stupid, Thea. Don't give away your secret. He'll wring your neck if he finds out you were behind that campaign.*

"I'm interested because I love animals—all animals. I don't understand how people can treat them like they don't feel or think," she said.

"Rabbits aren't humans," he said with a dismissive gesture.

"No, but they're worthy of respect. They can feel pain, fear—all the things we can feel."

"I don't torture animals for fun. No one does." Although his voice was level, she could hear the irritation growing.

"How is torturing animals for your benefit any different from doing it just for a sick kind of pleasure?" She wrapped her arms around herself. "You can't excuse it, no matter how you put it."

"Maybe not. And the funny thing is that I don't have to explain it to you. I don't have to explain my reasoning to anyone but myself and my board. The rest of you, who decide that you have an opinion without understanding the full scope of things, aren't my concern, because you'll never understand it."

"Like I said, maybe if you explain it, I'll understand it."

"I doubt that. Because like *I* said, I don't need to explain anything." A sneer crossed his face. "Do you think I built my company with people like you questioning my every move? Do you think I built my empire when every bleeding heart started wringing their hands? I had nothing, and I created this company myself. I was broke, starving while living in a dump, as I slaved away, knowing that if I kept going, I would make something of myself."

He stalked toward her, slowly backing her up, until she hit the wall behind her.

"I made something of myself," he said, "and I don't give two shits what you think about that. And I'm going to run my company as I see fit. Not how you see fit, not how anyone else sees as the best way. Do you understand *that?* Besides, there are other factors and laws at play here. It's not a black-and-white issue."

Thea frowned. "What other factors?"

"You call yourself some animal lover, but you don't do your research, do you?"

Thea flushed as he continued, "The only reason we continue to test on animals is because that's the only way to sell in the Chinese market. The government makes any foreign cosmetics companies comply with their laws. And if we were to save your precious rabbits and rats by pulling out of China, hundreds of people would be without jobs. So, how about you step down from your throne and stop judging people without understanding the full scope of things?"

Thea had known some of what Anthony spoke of, but if she were honest, she hadn't done as much research as she could have. She'd taken Mittens's word about how things were run, and she hadn't considered other countries' laws. She'd seen the photos of the animals in question, and she'd read about what was done to them.

"That still doesn't make it right," she said stubbornly. "You don't have to sell your stuff in China."

He let out a disgusted noise. "I'm not going to convince you what I'm doing is right or wrong. It isn't about that. It's about selling where there's a demand and giving people jobs. Can you say that you've done the same?"

Thea knew very well that she was baiting a bear when she said, "For someone who doesn't need to explain himself, you seem to need to explain yourself quite a lot."

Anthony didn't say anything. He did that thing where he stared down at her, like he was convinced she'd quiver and collapse at his feet. Too bad he seemed to forget that she wasn't the type of woman to do either of those things.

"And why do you care? What's your game?" He raked her with his gaze, like he could unravel her secrets. "Because if I didn't know better, I'd think you were one of the people trying to take me down."

Her heart seized in her chest. Doing her best to keep her voice steady, she said, "Now you're just paranoid."

He seemed to accept that answer. And when his lip curled

upward, Thea should have known that the last blow would fall like an axe to the neck.

"You're right," he said. "And the last thing I need is to listen to some washed-up wannabe artist who's too much of a coward to show anyone her stuff."

Her heart froze. "At least I haven't lost my humanity entirely," she whispered.

A moment later, he pushed away from the wall and stalked upstairs.

Thea covered her heart with her hand, willing it to stop pounding, and wishing that his words hadn't struck a nerve. Pain radiated through her. *Washed-up wannabe artist.* Tears burned in her eyes.

She'd wanted a reminder that he was an asshole, hadn't she? Well, she'd more than gotten that reminder.

CHAPTER TWELVE

Anthony didn't care what he'd have to sacrifice to get out of this cabin. He couldn't stay one more day with Thea and her incessant, prying questions. And he sure as hell couldn't keep seeing the hurt on her face after what he'd said to her.

He told himself it was for the best. Better that she hate him than want to reform him. He wasn't the type to be reformed. He didn't *want* to be reformed, dammit. He hadn't built one of the most powerful companies in the world by being nice.

Anthony called Cara and every person he could think of to get himself and Thea a way out of this cabin. He pulled strings; he called in favors. He wasn't above a bit of blackmail, either. By the end of the day, he'd secured a helicopter ride from a friend of another CEO who could land a helicopter in areas like this one. It wouldn't be easy, the pilot, Danny, had warned him, but he would try his best. At least the windstorm had died down.

Danny better come through, or Anthony was liable to do something really stupid. Like apologize to Thea.

He didn't tell her about their new travel arrangements. She didn't need to be aware of how much he wanted this entire debacle to be over. Besides, she might try to talk him out of it. That was the last thing he needed right now.

He needed to get back to work. He needed to stop thinking about how Thea felt, how he could've handled that conversation better. And he needed to stop wondering if she was more right than he cared to admit.

Anthony's thoughts of freedom were interrupted when his phone rang. Of course, things just had to go from bad to worse: it was Elise.

"Yes?" he answered.

"I heard about the flooding where you are. Are you still at the cabin?"

Anthony flicked a piece of lint from his shirt. "Why should you care? You'd still get your money even if I died."

"You're such an asshole. Can't I want to check in on you for no other reason than being worried?"

"No, you can't," was his deadpan reply.

Elise sighed. "Look, Tony, I didn't call to fight."

"You never do."

"I wanted to ask if you'd thought over what I talked to you about. About the money."

His grip tightened on his phone. "I already said it wasn't going to happen."

"I'm not asking for me, but for Ryan—"

At that, Anthony snarled, "Do you think I would *ever* do anything for that miserable son of a bitch who fucked my wife? Elise, if I thought you were delusional before, I now have confirmation."

"Ryan has been struggling to find work lately. I know you can change that."

"You already said you'd tell the press your secrets. So why haven't you done it?" he mocked.

She inhaled sharply. "Go to hell," she said. "If you had a heart at all—"

"You're right: I have no heart. Even if I did, I wouldn't spare even one ounce of it for you."

He hung up before she could reply. He knew Elise, and he knew she cared about her reputation almost more than she cared about money. He just hoped it stayed that way.

Anthony packed his things as he waited for Danny to call. But he didn't need to listen for his phone. When the helicopter flew over their cabin, you had to be deaf not to hear it.

Anthony headed outside. Thea already stood in the yard, looking up at the helicopter flying overhead.

"Is that…?" she asked, pointing.

"That's our ride. Get your stuff. We're leaving."

Thea gaped at him. Yelling over the sound of the helicopter, she said, "What? How? Were you going to tell me?"

"Either you can come now, or you can wait until somebody else decides to get you out of here."

"Seriously? You couldn't have asked me if I wanted to leave?"

"I didn't ask you because I'm not doing this for you. You can come, or you can stay. But *I'm* leaving."

He'd brought his suitcase downstairs already. Thea glared at him, her cheeks flushed with anger.

"What about my car?" she demanded. "I'm not just going to leave it here."

"I'm having two of my guys drive our cars down when they can. Until then, I'll pay for a rental car that you can use."

She opened her mouth, like she wanted to say no, but Anthony knew that she couldn't refuse a free rental car.

"You can stay, but who knows when you'll be able to drive out of here? It could be another week, maybe two. You'll run out of food." He smiled grimly. "You might have to eat Sneaky."

"I hate you, and I hope you get cholera." With that lovely statement, she went upstairs, presumably to pack her things.

Anthony could hear her moving about her room, and there were at least two instances where he thought he heard crashes. He was tempted to leave and let her figure out how to get to the helicopter, but he didn't need her scolding him during the ride home.

Thea finally came downstairs with her suitcase along with Sneaky in his cardboard box. "I need to get my food from the kitchen," she said, but Anthony caught her by the wrist.

"Don't worry about the food."

She stared at his fingers encircling her wrist, and it was like a brand burning into his skin. He let her go.

"Unlike you rich people, wasting food isn't something I do. It'll only take me a few minutes."

Anthony waited, tapping his foot with impatience as the minutes passed. He got a text from Danny. *I'm in a clearing about a half mile from the cabin. Are you coming?*

Anthony replied to the text with a curt affirmative. He was about to drag Thea from the kitchen when she finally came out with a bag of food. He took it from her before they finally headed out.

Silence reigned between them as they walked to the clearing. When Anthony realized that Thea was struggling to keep up with him, he shortened his strides. When she shot him an annoyed look, he ignored it.

Guilt gnawed at him. He wanted to tell her he shouldn't have ever touched her. He wanted to kiss her again, make her forget his harsh words. The temptation almost overwhelmed him when she stumbled a little, and he caught her just in time.

"All right?" he asked, helping her up.

Her hands were full of not only her suitcase, but the box carrying Sneaky. The rabbit had hidden away under multiple towels, probably terrified. He just hoped the towels were enough to muffle the sound of the helicopter.

She pulled away from him. "I'm fine. Let's go."

They didn't say another word to each other until they arrived at the helicopter.

The sound was deafening as they approached. Anthony helped Thea place her luggage and Sneaky inside before helping her up, climbing in beside her. Danny handed them both headsets. He yelled something that Anthony thought was a greeting.

Finally, they lifted into the air. Thea was turned away from him, gazing out the window as she held Sneaky's box in her lap. Anthony couldn't help but study her profile, the way her short blond hair curled at the ends. She had a smudge of dirt on her cheek, which he longed to wipe away.

His fingers curling into his palms, he stared straight ahead, telling himself that soon this would all be over. He would return to his life, and she would return to hers. They would never have to see each other again.

That thought should have comforted him. But for some reason, it only depressed him.

THEA STARED out the helicopter window, her shoulders slumping progressively further as they got closer to their destination. Would Anthony drop her off in Seattle, and she'd have to drive home? At this point, she wouldn't care if he dropped her off in New York City, as long as she got away from him.

The space in the back of the helicopter was cramped, and more than once, Thea's knee brushed his. The first time, she jerked away; the second time, he repositioned his legs so it wouldn't happen again.

Thea just hoped that this ride wouldn't terrify Sneaky to death. She could just make out his nose twitching under the pile of towels. She said a little prayer that she could get him home and then to a rescue afterward.

Out of the corner of her eye, she saw Anthony rub the back of his neck. His beard had grown in, making him seem more like a pirate than ever. She couldn't help but think about how he'd kissed her, the way his stubble had scraped at her cheeks and chin. How he'd touched her until she'd shattered in his arms.

It was humiliating, how attracted to him she still was. She told herself that attraction didn't have to go hand in hand with *liking* a person, but it was a small comfort. It made her feel weak and stupid. She wished she'd never met him in the first place.

They landed in a field about an hour later. It took Thea a moment to realize that they hadn't landed in Seattle, but on the outskirts of Fair Haven. Not far from the clearing were two cars waiting for them both. Thea saw one of the drivers get into the car in front, his face shaded by large sunglasses. She assumed that was the car Anthony would be riding in.

After both Anthony and Thea got out of the helicopter, Anthony yelled something at Danny before Danny took off again. Thea watched the helicopter until it was only a speck in the sky.

"You can use the rental car for however long it takes to get your car back," explained Anthony as he helped her with her luggage.

She placed Sneaky in the backseat and strapped him in for good measure. At Anthony's amused look, she rolled her eyes.

"Thanks," she said grudgingly. "Are you driving back to Seattle?"

"Yes."

"Then thanks for dropping me off near home."

Silence fell between them. It was strange, Thea thought, how they'd gotten so close yet there was this insurmountable wall between them now. Thea could almost convince herself the entire trip had been a bizarre nightmare that had, at times, become the sweetest of dreams.

Anthony stretched out his hand. "Good luck with everything."

She was rather tempted to reject his handshake and stomp on his foot instead. But she took his hand, shaking it quickly before she dropped it.

Anthony was about to open her car door for her, but Thea

stopped him. "Washed-up artists can get their own car doors," she said with a sarcastic smile.

His eyes darkened, but he didn't defend himself. Instead, after she'd climbed inside her car, he closed her car door with such a light touch that it only irritated Thea further.

And then Thea was driving away, Anthony getting smaller and smaller in her rearview mirror, before disappearing entirely.

She barely remembered arriving home. Focusing solely on Sneaky, she got the rabbit inside, finding a much larger box to set him in. She got him fresh water and food before she began to call rescues in the area. To her relief, one said they'd take him when they opened the next morning.

After taking a long shower, she collapsed into bed, falling asleep in the middle of the afternoon and not waking until the sun had already set.

CHAPTER THIRTEEN

Anthony stared into his glass of beer before drinking the entire glass in one long gulp.

"That bad, huh?" his good friend Carter Roberts asked with a grimace.

A pro baseball player for the Seattle Falcons, Carter always had a posse of fans following him around wherever he went. Tonight was no different. He'd already taken at least five photos with people, and Anthony could see a group of girls ogling him at the table behind them. It would only be a few more minutes before they got the courage to approach one of the most famous baseball players in the country and one of the most eligible bachelors around.

One of the girls, a brunette who was so tan that she looked orange, stepped up to their table with a giggle. "Are you Carter Roberts?" she asked breathlessly, like she didn't already know the answer.

Carter shot her a grin. "I am. But the more important question is: who are you?"

The girl tittered. Anthony snorted and motioned at the waitress to bring him another beer.

Carter and the girl—who was soon joined by her two friends—chatted, the girls mostly giggling. Finally, they took a group selfie and returned to their booth.

Carter possessed easy good looks that made him seem like the ultimate American boy next door. It helped that he was one of the best pitchers in the league. Because of a shoulder injury, he hadn't played this season, though, and Anthony knew Carter was itching to get back into the game. Carter tended to do stupid things when he was bored and stuck on the bench, a situation he hadn't experienced since college.

"Are you done yet?" said Anthony. "Because I'm feeling like a third wheel tonight."

"You're always a third wheel. Besides, they're just excited. They don't mean any harm."

"Doesn't make them less annoying."

Carter snorted. "This is why people hate you and like me."

Anthony couldn't disagree with that assessment. Carter had always wanted to be loved, while Anthony had only wanted to be feared.

They'd known each other since high school, and Carter had been the one person in Anthony's life to stick by him through the years. They'd both lived in the same dorm in college with Ryan Weaver, and after the Ryan and Elise thing, Carter had stuck by Anthony.

Anthony still didn't understand why Carter had stayed friends with him, though. It wasn't as if Anthony was a good friend. Maybe it was just stubbornness on Carter's part. Or a stupid kind of loyalty that Anthony would never fully understand.

But they'd been friends since Carter had decided that Anthony should be a part of his cool kids clique when Anthony had preferred his own company. Carter was one of those people who didn't take no for an answer when he decided you were going to be in his life.

"People liking me hasn't gotten me to where I am now," said Anthony prosaically.

"Well, if your goal was to be disliked, you've definitely accomplished it. How many of your board members want your head on a platter now?"

Anthony smiled grimly. "Only one, officially. And it's only because of Ryan."

Carter was one of the few people who knew what had really happened between Anthony and Elise. He shook his head. "I wouldn't trade places with you for all the money in the world."

When Carter had texted him to get drinks, Anthony had almost declined because he knew Carter would want to hear about his disastrous vacation-turned-nightmare. It had been two weeks since he'd returned home, and during that entire time, he hadn't been able to get Thea out of his head.

He saw her on the streets of Seattle. Once, he'd seen a woman with short blond hair and had almost called Thea's name, only to realize the woman wasn't Thea at all. He saw her when he passed by the seemingly endless array of vegan restaurants downtown. When Cara mentioned that she was thinking of getting a pet rabbit, he was almost convinced there was some conspiracy to keep him from forgetting Thea.

Would he never forget about the damn woman? He didn't

need this distraction, to say the least. He hadn't been this obsessed with a woman since Elise, and even then, he'd focused more on building his company to impress Elise than he had thought about Elise herself.

"At least I'm not fawned over wherever I go." Anthony scowled when another group of girls noticed Carter as they came into the bar. "Can you tell them to calm down?"

Carter shrugged. "They mean well. And the ones who really mean well are great to have around, if you know what I mean." Carter's expression sobered. "So, you still haven't told me all about this cabin excursion turned horror movie. I'm surprised you made it out alive."

"Not as surprised as I am." Anthony took a long drink of his third beer that night. He exhaled slowly. "I basically got stuck in a cabin with the most obnoxious woman in the history of the universe. She almost killed me. Literally."

Carter's eyebrows shot straight to his hairline. "Now that's a story."

Anthony related the tale, with the only interruptions being fans wanting Carter's autograph or a photo with him. Eventually, Anthony began to scowl at anyone stupid enough to approach their table. They could wait until he'd finished talking, dammit.

"She was the craziest woman I've ever met," he said, now on his fourth beer. "She thinks eating meat is evil. She almost got herself killed trying to save a rabbit. A motherfucking *rabbit*. Who does that? And then she has all these notebooks of her artwork that she refuses to let anyone else see. Again, who does that?"

Carter's lip twitched. "She sounds interesting," was his rather deadpan reply.

"Interesting? I should've pushed her into the creek when I had the chance."

His words were halfhearted, though. He thought of their kiss in the hallway, how she'd melted in his arms, moaned his name. How free she was with her affection, and how she blossomed like a flower in the sunshine with physical touch. He thought of how she laughed, how she talked to Sneaky the rabbit like it could understand her. Mostly he could still feel the shape of her as she'd perched on his lap, and how she'd come under his hand without an ounce of inhibition.

"So you really helped her save that rabbit?" Carter eyed him, an odd expression on his face. "You, Anthony Bertram, who doesn't care about anything but money and himself?"

"I told you: she would've drowned or broken her neck if I hadn't."

"She sounds smart enough to figure it out on her own." Carter sipped his own drink in a thoughtful silence.

Irritated at his friend's smug smile, Anthony muttered, "Just fucking say it, man."

"I don't have anything to say."

"Bullshit. You have the most to say of anyone I've ever met besides Thea herself."

"Well, it's been, what, two weeks since you got back from this trip? And I've never known you to think about any one woman longer than it takes you to get her home and get into her pants."

"Pot, meet kettle," said Anthony dryly.

Carter held up his hands, laughing. "I'm not judging you. I'm just making an observation—"

"Somehow I doubt that's all this is."

"An *observation* that you can't stop talking about this

woman, and the fact that she irritated you this much means she got under your skin." Carter smiled so widely that Anthony wanted to punch him in the face. "You like her, don't you?"

"Just because I wanted to fuck her doesn't mean I liked her."

"But you didn't fuck her. You said it yourself."

"Okay, so what? It just means I need to get her out of my system. I didn't get what I wanted, and I still want it."

Carter frowned. "Maybe. But if you just want sex, you could find lots of other women to fill that hole." He chuckled at his dirty pun.

Anthony stared down at his beer, surprised that he only had a little bit left of this one. He'd never been a huge drinker, at least not to the point of getting drunk, but tonight apparently all bets were off. He was talking to Carter like they were teenage girls in a romcom and he was chugging down beer like it was water from a desert oasis. What the hell was wrong with him?

He curled his fingers into a fist. *Thea.* It was all her fault.

Maybe he'd already come up with his own answer to the problem: he just needed to fuck her properly. He'd scratch the itch, and then he'd move on. She'd only be another name on a long list—nothing more, nothing less.

"Look, I'm hardly the best guy to give advice on love and shit," said Carter, "but I saw how you were after the Elise thing. I know you like to act like you're some heartless bastard, but nobody is really heartless, least of all you."

"Since when did you turn into Oprah?" said Anthony, asperity dripping from his voice.

"Maybe since I injured my shoulder and everything I

thought was going to happen didn't. Maybe I'm drunk." Carter leaned forward until only a few inches separated the two men.

"But maybe meeting this woman has shown you that maybe you don't really want a shallow bitch like Elise. Maybe you actually do like her. Maybe you actually have *feelings*." Carter chuckled; he must be drunk, too.

Anthony stared at his friend, thinking over Carter's words, before he put his hand on Carter's forehead and pushed him away.

"I'm not nearly drunk enough to listen to this," said Anthony. He finished off his beer and waved at their waitress. "So let me get drunk first before you start reciting sonnets and crying over romance novels."

Carter just laughed. Then another group of girls recognized him and effectively distracted Carter long enough for Anthony to get his thoughts back in order.

But Carter's words stuck in his brain no matter how much he wanted to ignore them. It irritated him that his friend was probably right. Anthony wasn't particularly fond of people pointing out his mistakes. It made him seem weak and foolish.

After the latest group of fans departed, Anthony asked, "What's new with you?"

"You're changing the subject, but I'll let you. For now." Carter's usual easy grin faded. "Nothing much to tell. My PT isn't sure my shoulder will be healed enough for me to return in the fall."

Anthony grimaced. "Shit, I didn't know. It's that bad?"

"Apparently. I'm not about to get benched again, but if my PT won't sign off on me returning, there's not much I can do."

Anthony knew very well that without baseball, Carter was lost. He'd been playing for most of his life, and when he'd signed with the pros, it had been a dream come true. Carter had become the player that he'd always said he would be, but if he could no longer play…

"I thought we were getting drinks to relax, not talk about our sad, pathetic lives," said Anthony. He tried to make it sound like a joke, but between his own confusion around Thea and Carter's glum expression, neither man ended up laughing.

After that, Anthony stuck with topics that weren't as depressing. It helped that they kept the drinks flowing. When a previous group of fans returned, Carter invited them to sit with them, which lightened the mood considerably. Although most of the women focused their attentions on Carter, a brunette with curves for days set her sights on Anthony.

"I know you," she said, her voice like liquid honey. She pushed her hair over her shoulder, and it gleamed in the low light. "You're that businessman, aren't you?"

He took in the brunette. Her breasts were on full display in her ridiculously tight blouse. Normally, Anthony would've taken her up on her obvious invitation. But tonight, he found himself bored by her. And that rankled him more than anything else that night.

I'm not going to let Thea control me like this, he vowed. *I'll never let any woman sink her claws into me again.*

Anthony shot the brunette a seductive smile. "You're not interested in Carter Roberts's illustrious autograph?"

The brunette smiled, her white teeth flashing. Leaning toward Anthony, her breasts brushing his arm, she whispered, "I have a confession: I don't care about baseball."

Anthony whispered back, "Neither do I."

She giggled. She smelled like roses, all sweetness and femininity. When she touched his arm with light fingers, his body responded. He considered taking her home with him, yet the prospect didn't excite him. It was such a depressing thought that he finished his last drink, paid for his check, and told Carter he was heading out.

The brunette frowned in confusion, her lower lip protruding forward. Anthony ignored her. He smiled grimly when he heard her mutter *asshole* as he walked away.

That night at his penthouse, he stared into the fire lit in his office, brooding. He thought about what Carter had said, that maybe he wanted something that wasn't Elise. Maybe he wasn't such a heartless bastard, despite what Thea had said.

He remembered how Thea had looked at him when he'd rescued the rabbit. He remembered the hurt in her eyes when he'd insulted her—twice. And he remembered the way she'd responded when he'd kissed her, and how she was unlike any other woman he'd ever met. There was an innocence and a purity about her that had enchanted him. She wore her heart on her sleeve and didn't care what others thought.

What would it be like to have a woman with a heart as kind as hers to care about him? The thought was almost unbearable, so he pushed it away. *Let her go. Let this go, man.*

For the rest of the night, he gazed into the fire until the wood was just ashes and the fire dissipated entirely.

CHAPTER FOURTEEN

Thea usually loved spending time with her family—usually being the operative word. Tonight, however, she wanted nothing more than to go home and be alone.

It all started when Trent's wife Lizzie invited Thea over for dinner. Considering that Thea had pleaded exhaustion twice already for previous dinner invitations since returning from her disastrous vacation, she'd known she couldn't decline a third time without her siblings banging down her door, demanding to know what was wrong.

Now Thea sat at dinner with Trent, Lizzie, and their three-year-old daughter, Bea, along with Ash and his girlfriend, Violet Fielding.

Trent owned three restaurants in Fair Haven and planned to open another one in Seattle in the next year. Lizzie, one of the illustrious Thorntons of Fair Haven, had grown up with a silver spoon in her mouth, but Thea appreciated that Lizzie hadn't inherited her parents' snooty ways. Lizzie had gone on tour with her band last fall, Trent and Bea coming along for a part of it, essentially roughing it the entire time. Thea was hardly an expert singer, but even she could recognize talent when Lizzie sang and played.

Ash was Thea's younger brother, and they'd been the closest in age growing up. Ash had recently settled down with Violet, to everyone's immense surprise, considering his playboy past. Violet, a widow five years older than Ash, had somehow tamed the beast and left him happier for it. Thea liked Violet's no-nonsense attitude and how she managed Ash, usually with nothing more than a smile and a raised eyebrow.

Trent had dinner brought in from his tapas restaurant, La Bonita. Thea's stomach rumbled when she smelled the array of dishes set on the table: steamed mussels, crusty bread with olive tapenade, spicy fried potatoes, and chicken skewers with a bright red pepper sauce, among other dishes. Thea didn't know how they'd eat all of this food, but then again, her brothers could eat their weight and go back for seconds and thirds, too.

"The bread is vegan," said Trent with a wry smile. "Don't worry, little sis, I have you covered."

She smiled. "Since when did you make that change?"

"Since somebody complained that bread could be vegan and why wasn't ours?"

Ash took a bite of chicken with gusto. "You're missing out. But you already knew that." He swallowed and sighed with pleasure. "I love meat."

Violet snorted. "We all know how much you love meat. And everything else that's going to give you a heart attack someday."

He patted his chest with a bright smile. "Healthy as a horse. Sorry, you're not getting rid of me that easily."

Bea, in her highchair next to Lizzie, was given some

cheese, along with small bites of the chicken. When Lizzie began to eat one of the mussels, Bea said, "I want some!"

Lizzie raised an eyebrow. "You sure? I don't know if you'll like it, baby."

Bea leaned over, trying to reach the mussel in her mother's hand. Thea bit back a laugh as Lizzie scooped the mussel out of the shell and placed it on Bea's tray. The toddler scooped it up and ate it, chewing thoughtfully. The adults all seemed to hold their breaths. Then Bea swallowed the mussel and returned to her chicken without another word.

Lizzie laughed. "She won't eat broccoli, but she'll eat a mussel. Of course."

"She has expensive tastes," joked Trent, kissing Bea on her rosy cheek.

Thea watched her family eat and laugh, glad that two of her brothers had found happiness. Trent had been so burdened with caring for them all, only to be haunted by how he hadn't done enough for their mother, that Thea was glad that he'd let go of a lot of the past to be with Lizzie. He and Lizzie had been star-crossed lovers, falling head over heels for each other in high school, only to break up and not see each other again for many years.

As they ate, they passed around a pitcher of red sangria. To Thea's surprise, Lizzie declined a glass, preferring to sip water.

I bet Lizzie has a secret, she thought, smiling to herself.

"So, Thea, tell us all about your trip," said Violet after they'd all eaten so much that Thea was sure her stomach would burst. "I want to hear all about it. You were really stuck in a cabin with some strange guy for days?"

"Not just some strange guy," said Ash, "but Anthony Bertram."

Violet frowned. "Am I supposed to know who that is?"

"He's a billionaire. Makes more money sitting on the can than we can dream of making in our lifetimes." At Violet's continued confused expression, Ash added, "Pretty sure his company makes those bath things you love."

Her eyes lit up. "Oh! Really? Well, no wonder he's rich."

"Yes, tell us all about this rich guy you got stranded with," drawled Trent.

Thea ignored her brother's wry tone. If she'd been cagey about telling them all about what had happened, well, could they blame her? She'd needed time to process everything.

The morning after she'd arrived back in Fair Haven, she'd taken Sneaky to a wildlife rescue. She'd related the story of how she and Anthony had saved Sneaky. The rescue woman had stared at her in astonishment as Thea had told the story. At the end of Thea's recital, the woman had blurted, "This guy must really like you to do something like that."

Thea had chosen not to respond to that remark, instead asking questions about Sneaky and his prospects of healing and being released back into the wild. Although the woman couldn't guarantee anything, she did say that his chances seemed good, considering that his injury was healing. But they wouldn't know for sure until they looked him over thoroughly.

After leaving Sneaky at the rescue, Thea had driven home with tears in her eyes. It was stupid, to be crying over a rabbit, but she'd gotten attached to him.

Or maybe she'd cried because Sneaky had been the last link to Anthony. Now, with Sneaky gone, it was truly over. And that thought had been so depressing that she'd cried for an hour before getting dressed and driving herself to work.

Since then, she'd gotten her own car back, cleaner and shinier than she'd ever seen it. The man who'd dropped off her car had handed her an envelope with a single piece of paper inside that had read: *Hope the rabbit made it. Anthony.*

Thea had wanted to drive straight down to Seattle and find Anthony herself, and—well, she didn't know what she'd do. Slap him, probably. Throw his stupid note in his face. Maybe throw some more of his sandwiches out the window.

And she might just kiss him. Which meant that staying put in Fair Haven, miles away from him, was the best thing she could do to get over him.

Thea realized she hadn't answered Trent's question, and she blushed as her family stared at her. Only Bea didn't care, too interested in eating cubes of cheese. At least the three-year-old wasn't judging her, Thea thought.

"There's not much to tell about the trip," said Thea, shrugging. "The weather was terrible and the storm washed away the bridge. Then there was a mix-up with the reservations. It was basically a comedy of errors with a side of power outages."

"I hope you got a refund," said Trent seriously.

"Ted gave us both refunds and a free voucher for another stay at a later date." Thea smiled wryly. "Although I'm not sure I'll ever take him up on it, given what happened the first time."

"But what was Anthony Bertram like?" said Lizzie. At Trent's raised eyebrow, she blushed a little. "What? Anthony Bertram is one of the most eligible bachelors around. Just because I'm married doesn't mean I'm blind."

"Now I'm going to have to go beat this guy up," said Trent, only half-joking.

Lizzie patted him on the arm. "No chance of me leaving you. The food's too good."

Lizzie laughed when Trent growled, and for a moment, everyone was too distracted by the general revelry to press Thea. She took a deep breath and drank her sangria, hoping they wouldn't keep asking her questions.

But that would've been too good to be true. Trent and Ash began to double down on their interrogation. When Thea revealed that Anthony had orchestrated the entire trip home without consulting her, they were angry on her behalf.

"He didn't even ask you?" demanded Ash. "And you just went along with it?"

"He sounds like a shithead. I'm sorry you got stuck with him," said Trent.

Thea decided not to mention the whole kissing thing. Or the arguments. Or how she was also behind the viral campaign that had seriously damaged Anthony's company's image… no, Thea would take those secrets to her grave.

"Well, what was she supposed to do?" Violet countered. "What if she'd gotten stuck there for even longer? That would've been terrible."

Ash crossed his arms. "He sounds like a heavy-handed son of a bitch who needs a good thrashing."

Violet rolled her eyes. "Like you aren't heavy-handed."

While Ash and Violet bickered over that particular comment, Lizzie leaned toward Thea to whisper, "Something else happened, didn't it?"

Thea stilled. Looking up, she could see the sparkle in Lizzie's eyes.

Damn her for being so perceptive.

Not remotely wanting to spill her secrets to her brothers or their significant others, Thea said, "And what about you? You're not drinking, even though I know you love sangria."

Guilt assailed Thea immediately. Luckily, Lizzie just laughed, good sport that she was.

"Maybe I'm just on a diet," she said, but her smile was only getting wider.

"Ah, come on, just tell 'em. You're already past the first trimester," said Trent.

At the word *trimester,* the entire table erupted. Violet gasped and hugged Lizzie, while Ash chuckled before shaking Trent's hand. Thea also gave Lizzie a hug, amazed that despite Lizzie's petite size, she couldn't see any kind of baby bump yet. Then again, it was early still.

"Yes, I'm pregnant"—Violet interrupted with a squeal —"and I'm due in October. Right before Halloween, actually." She rubbed her belly. "I'm sorry we didn't tell you all sooner, but I'm a worrywart and wanted to wait."

Thea knew that Lizzie had had a miscarriage in her first trimester before Bea, so she couldn't blame them both for keeping mum.

"To the next generation of Youngers," said Ash as he raised his glass. Everyone cheered and toasted.

After the dinner, Thea went outside on the back porch for a moment to herself, only for Violet to follow her. Violet shot her a sympathetic smile.

"I'm not going to ask if you want to talk about what happened, except to say if you *do* want to talk, I'll listen and won't comment. And I won't tell Ash, either."

Thea snorted. "I'm going to have to get that in writing. Maybe in blood, too."

"Hey, I can keep a secret from your brother. Besides, just because I love him doesn't mean I agree with everything he thinks. Since I only have a sister, I never knew how protective brothers could be."

"Protective? More like nosy and obnoxious."

"They mean well."

Thea knew that, and she loved her brothers with all her heart. As the silence wrapped around her and Violet, she found herself wanting to tell somebody about her crazy adventure in the woods. About how she couldn't get this man out of her mind. How she dreamed of Anthony Bertram almost every night. It was like he haunted her.

In quiet tones, she gave in to the urge. She related the entire story—the mix-up, the rabbit, the kissing, Anthony's cruel words to her—and Thea was thankful that Violet just listened.

By the time Thea was done, she needed Violet to say something. Was she judging Thea for being an idiot? Thea wouldn't blame her, but it was still a depressing thought.

"You know, when your brother and I were together," Violet began, her voice thoughtful, "I was convinced he was just some playboy. He wasn't a bad guy, of course, but he wasn't exactly what I'd call relationship material. But when I looked below the surface, I saw things that showed me that I was wrong."

Thea sighed. "So what are you saying?"

"I don't know." Violet laughed quietly. "Only that it's obvious Anthony showed a different side of himself to you. A side I would bet he doesn't show just anybody. That, I think, counts for a lot."

Thea wrapped her arms around herself. If Anthony cared about her, why would he have said those things to her? *A washed-up wannabe artist.* She still cringed when she heard those words in her head. But she'd also attacked his business and ethics, so she almost couldn't blame him for lashing out.

Almost, but not quite.

"I think I'm in a muddle," said Thea, groaning. "I don't know what to do and it pisses me off."

Violet patted her on the arm. "Nobody knows what to do when it comes to these kinds of things. You'll figure it out. And I would also bet that this Anthony guy will show up when you least expect it, because who could forget somebody like you?"

"I'm sad that you're with my brother, because clearly we would make a great couple," joked Thea.

Violet laughed. They hugged briefly before returning inside when Ash popped his head out to ask what they were gossiping about.

Thea arrived home and poured herself a glass of wine, mulling over what Violet had said. She wondered if she'd already forgiven Anthony for what he'd said to her. Did that make her weak? She smiled wryly, thinking of how she'd given him that speech about forgiveness.

No, she hadn't forgiven him, but she still wanted to see him. Thus was her conundrum. Too bad in all of the chaos she hadn't gotten his number. All she knew was that he lived in Seattle in what she guessed was some ridiculously expensive high-rise apartment. Or maybe some mansion that overlooked

Puget Sound. She didn't even want to imagine how much he paid every month for his living situation.

Thea was about to go to bed—or drink another glass of wine, she wasn't sure yet—when a knock on her front door almost made her drop her wineglass. Her heart pounding, she waited, wondering if the person had gotten the wrong door. Who was here this late at night?

Another knock, this one louder.

Then, a voice. "Thea, I know you're in there. Let me in."

She couldn't believe it. It was Anthony.

No, it couldn't be.

She rushed to the door, wrenching it open. And to her absolute shock, Anthony Bertram himself really was standing on her doorstep, his expression thunderous.

"What—?" said Thea.

But she didn't get a chance to finish that sentence. In the next moment, Anthony pushed inside her apartment, wrapped her in his arms, and kissed her.

CHAPTER FIFTEEN

T hea wondered if she'd fallen asleep and was dreaming that Anthony was here, kissing her as fiercely as he'd kissed her that first time. And the second time. His hands skimmed down her back and cupped her ass as his tongue delved into her mouth.

No, this definitely isn't a dream. It's all real.

Thea could barely put two coherent thoughts together right then. But one single thought did come to the foray: what was he even doing here at her apartment?

She put her hands on his chest, pushing at him. He finally broke the kiss, although he didn't step away from her.

Thea swallowed. Her voice none too steady, she said, "Why are you here?"

"Do you really want to talk right now?" He slid an arm around her waist, pulling her close again. "Because I don't want to talk, Thea."

She was tempted to give in. God, was she tempted. He looked delicious, with his dark eyes looking at her with such heat that she was pretty sure she would go up in flames in the next few seconds. He wore a dark sweater that delineated his muscular body, and Thea wanted to put her hands all over him. She sighed inwardly. She wished he had a huge wart on his nose, or bad breath, or something *human* that she could use as a reason that she shouldn't be attracted to him in the first place.

Thea shook her head and took a step back. Folding her arms across her chest, she said, "You can't just come to my apartment without even telling me, bang on my door, kiss me, and then act like telling me why you're here is too much to ask."

Anthony clenched his jaw. Pushing his fingers through his hair, he replied, "I wanted to finish what we started. That's all."

"You drove all the way from Seattle—where I'm going to assume there are plenty of women for you to sleep with—just for sex?" Thea rolled her eyes. "I don't have time for whatever this is. And before you so rudely interrupted me, I was going to go to sleep. Because that's what normal people do at eleven at night."

She waited for him to tell her that he'd missed her, or that he was sorry for what he'd said to her. And then the inevitable guilt nipped at her, because it wasn't like she was the only injured party here, either.

If you really care about him, you should tell him the truth. Before you go any further with this. It's wrong not to.

Wrong, yes, but Thea decided that until Anthony explained himself, she wouldn't say a word to him about her involvement in that pesky social media campaign. If her conscience got upset at her for that decision, she muffled it and did her best to ignore it.

Thea sighed. "Why are you really here, Anthony? Be honest for once. You might enjoy the feeling."

He looked so irritated with her that she had to stifle laughter. She had a feeling that Anthony Bertram wasn't the type of man to let himself be vulnerable, which saddened her in a way, too. You couldn't truly connect with any person if you were unwilling to pull down the wall you erected to keep yourself from getting hurt.

"I couldn't get you out of my mind," he finally admitted.

Thea raised an eyebrow. "And?"

"And? What else is there to explain?"

"I guess it's a bit of a leap to go from 'can't stop thinking about this person' to 'driving in the middle of the night to her apartment without telling her.'"

"Like I said—I needed to see you."

His lips quirked, and Thea couldn't stop the frisson of heat that bloomed inside her at the sight. God, she'd missed that stupid, arrogant smile of his. She must have some kind of brain damage to miss a guy like him. Maybe she had actually fallen into the creek and was now a vegetable, dreaming of a man who she could never have.

He sighed. "Do you want me to leave or not?"

Thea was tempted to kick him out, but her curiosity got the better of her. "Since you're here, you might as well come in for a drink. Although I have to warn you, I only buy cheap wine. Nothing fancy around here."

Anthony glanced around her apartment, a one-bedroom that she'd decorated in bright colors to make it seem more inviting. It was small, of course, probably the size of one of his many closets. He picked up a brochure from the counter from the wildlife rescue she'd taken Sneaky to.

"What happened to the rabbit?" he asked as he followed her into her tiny kitchen.

"A rescue group took him. Last email I got from them, he was close to being healed enough to be released back into the wild."

Thea poured herself a glass of wine and another for Anthony. He took it without comment, although he grimaced after he took a single sip.

"This stuff is terrible," he said, coughing a little. "It's like sour piss water."

"Like I said: I don't have rich people tastes. Or rich people money." She smiled, sipping her own glass of wine. "I can always get you a glass of water, since you're such a lightweight."

Her dig prompted him to continue drinking his own glass of wine. Let it never be said that Anthony Bertram would let a dare pass, Thea thought sardonically.

They eventually wandered into the living room. Anthony stood and looked at her artwork on the walls.

"This is your stuff?" he said.

"Yes." A lot of it was drawings from years ago, some from her brief stint at art school before she'd dropped out. Although Thea hated to show her art to people, having it on her walls didn't bother her. Perhaps it was because it was from a time long ago, when she'd almost been another person. Or maybe it was because it was rare that she had guests, besides her siblings, who knew well enough not to ask questions about her failed art career.

Anthony, though, wasn't one of her brothers. He pointed to a painting she'd done right after graduating from high school: it was all swirls of color, a sort of Impressionistic version of a sunset. Thea had always loved that painting.

"I thought you didn't let anyone else see your art," Anthony said. "You got pretty heated when I found your drawings in the cabin."

"That's because you came into my room without asking."

"I doubt it was just that."

She shrugged. "It's hard to explain. Besides, these are all old pieces. I don't paint anymore. I prefer my graphic novels."

Anthony continued to gaze at her painting. "I've seen enough overpriced artwork to know when someone is actually talented. And you're one of those people. It's a waste not to share this with the world."

"Did you come here to talk about my art? Because you could've just called. I'm going to assume you could've gotten my number, too."

He set his wineglass down on the coffee table. He then plucked her glass from her fingers and said, "We both know why I'm here. And if you had really wanted me to leave, you would've kicked me out by now."

She couldn't disagree with that. When he cupped the back of her neck, she beat him to the punch: she put her hands on his shoulders, stood on her tiptoes, and kissed him herself.

He stilled, surprised, before wrapping his arms around her as he deepened the kiss. He groaned. Thea's heart almost burst in her chest at that sound. It was a sound of his surrender, one she felt echoed in her own body.

It felt right, being in his arms. But before she could let this go any further, she broke the kiss and said, "I'm still mad at you, you know. For what you said."

His eyes flashed. "You're still a huge pain in the ass," he countered.

She laughed. "Fair enough."

After that, there wasn't any more reason to talk.

Thea led him to her bedroom, although both of them were more concerned with stripping out of their clothes with so much haste that the garments flew in every direction. Thea burst out laughing when her shirt hit her bedside lamp, almost toppling it to the floor.

"If you break my stuff, you're going to have to replace it," she said.

His dark eyes gleamed. "Anything to get you under me."

She shivered, and she shivered even more when he kissed her throat. His lips traveled a path to her shoulder, nipping at the tendon there. She ran her fingers through his hair. She couldn't help being delighted at how soft the strands were. She had a feeling it was the only soft thing about him.

Anthony reached behind her and unclasped her bra without missing a beat. She wanted to joke about his bra-taking-off abilities, but then when he kissed her again, all jokes fled her mind.

He cupped her breasts, the calluses on his fingers providing delicious friction. When he rolled one nipple between thumb and forefinger, she let out a startled moan.

"I didn't get to see these properly last time," he said. "It was too dark."

He moved so that he sat on the bed while she stood in front of him, her breasts now at the level of his mouth—a mouth that he put to extremely good use.

He sucked and licked her breasts until Thea almost melted into a puddle at his feet. When he bit down lightly on one nipple, she gasped, her fingers digging into his scalp.

"Your tits are gorgeous, by the way. And your nipples are as red as berries now." He licked her sternum before kissing her over her pounding heart.

"I always thought they were too small."

"No. Never." His eyes were serious, but playful. "Don't ever change them."

She giggled, and then she laughed harder when he pulled her down onto her bed. They tangled together, rolling across the sheets, before Anthony pinned her beneath him. She helped him strip her of the rest of her clothing until she was naked. She pouted up at him when she realized that he still wore his jeans.

"Why am I naked and you're not?" she whined, pulling at his belt. But he pushed her hands away.

"Because I want to savor you, and if I'm naked, it'll be three seconds before I'm inside you."

Well, she wouldn't complain if that were the case. As Anthony kissed down her torso and swirled his tongue in her belly button, she also had to admit that she liked this whole savoring thing.

She'd had good sex before, and she'd had mediocre sex before. Her last boyfriend had been decent in bed, although he hadn't been much for kissing and tended to fall asleep right afterward, whereas Thea was always wired and ready to go after sex.

But Anthony treated her like she was something worth taking his time with. She understood now why so many women had thrown themselves at him. The man knew his way around a woman's body. The thought of other women experiencing his kisses and touch caused a twinge of jealousy that she ruthlessly pushed away. This wasn't going to be more than a fling—as long as she remembered that, she wouldn't get her heart broken.

But it was difficult to remember that when Anthony kissed her pelvis, skimming a light touch from her upper thigh to her hipbone. She wiggled.

"Ticklish?" he asked.

"Yes—no, no, stop!"

He tickled her some more until she begged for mercy. Trying to catch her breath, she almost didn't realize that he'd parted her legs until she felt his mouth, hot and wet, kissing the insides of her thighs. Already pulsing with need, she arched upward, wordlessly telling him what she wanted.

He kissed her mound, but he didn't kiss her where she wanted him the most. Gripping his hair, she tried to guide him. He just laughed in a low voice.

"Why am I not surprised that you'd be demanding in bed?" said Anthony. His gaze caught hers as he stroked her hip with gentle fingers.

"And I should've known that you'd be a jerk here, too."

That just made him shake his head, and before she could protest, he moved down her legs. He kissed her shins, rubbing at a mole on her left calf. He kissed one ankle and then the next, and Thea almost came out of her skin when he bit the delicate skin there.

Finally, he moved where she ached for him most. He pushed her legs apart until he could feast his eyes upon her glistening sex. His voice was a rumbling purr as he said, "You're already so wet and I've barely touched you."

She rolled her eyes at how proud he sounded, but she didn't care that he was so arrogant when he parted her and licked her in one slow motion. Her toes curled into her comforter as he feasted upon her. She felt her blood pounding in her veins as he licked and kissed her, his tongue dancing around her clit just to drive her even more insane. She was already close to falling over the edge.

"Damn, you're sweet. You taste like lemons here, too," he said roughly.

"Aren't lemons sour?" Her mind was hazy and slow.

He pushed a finger inside her, making her moan. "You taste like sweet lemons," he amended, his eyes gleaming.

Then he fastened his lips on her clit, and soon her entire world fell away. All she could think and feel and smell and see was Anthony. The combined movement of his finger inside her sheath and his mouth on her clit sent her straight into her release. She cried out, bowing upward, and Anthony had to push on her hips to keep her on the bed.

She panted for a while, trying to order her thoughts. When he shot her a lazy, arrogant smile, she knew she wanted to make him as crazed for her as she was for him.

Pushing him down onto the bed, she got on top of him. His eyes darkened.

"Fair is fair," she said as she touched his chest. She hadn't seen as much of him as she'd liked, and her mouth watered as she took in his muscles, the dark hair scattered across his chest, and the way his breath made his trim stomach concave upon inhalation. She touched his sides, which made him jump. She laughed.

"So you're ticklish, too? Good to know." She danced her

fingers along his right side until he was grabbing at her errant hands and holding her still.

"Didn't I tell you that you're playing with fire, Thea?" he growled.

"I like fire." She shot him an impish grin as she unbuckled his belt and pushed his jeans down his legs. Her mouth watered, seeing how aroused he was already. Her heart pounded as she unveiled his cock. It was a glorious sight: long and thick and veined, and when she leaned down to lick the tip, she tasted salt.

Anthony swore under his breath, but he didn't try to take over. He put his hands on her neck as she licked and sucked. She loved the way he grew harder with each swipe of her tongue. She fondled his balls. He groaned, and then just a moment later, he flipped her over until she was under him again.

"Enough." He kissed her like a wild man. She wrapped her arms and legs around him. His cock pressed against her dripping sex, but before Anthony could slide home, he growled, "Condom?"

Condom. Yes, condoms. Thea's dazed mind barely registered the request as she reached inside her bedside drawer and pulled out a silver packet. She hadn't used one in ages, but thank God she never cleaned out her drawers. She probably had lip balms and hair ties in there from ten years ago. At least she knew these condoms weren't that old. Anthony took the packet from her with a seductive smile.

"I'm surprised you don't carry one in your wallet," she said.

He snorted. "I'm not a teenage boy hoping to score."

As he rolled the condom down his cock, she thought, *No, you're not, thank God.*

He kissed her again, the kiss demanding something of her that she didn't know if she was ready to give. Then Anthony was pushing inside her, slowly, taking his time, letting her get used to him. Her heart contracted as he filled her, and by the time he was seated fully inside her, she felt like her entire soul was full of him.

Thea touched his cheeks and his jaw, and when he turned his head to kiss her palm, she wanted to cry. It was just a fling —right?

He hadn't moved yet, simply letting Thea touch him for a while. "Good?" he asked, his voice guttural.

She arched upward, and they both groaned. Like fire sparking along her veins, she suddenly needed all that he could give her. She dragged her foot along his leg and said, "I need you. So much."

Anthony pulled out before thrusting into her, slowly but deftly, her nerve endings singing with each movement he made. Thea closed her eyes, pleasure searing her veins with each stroke of his cock. He muttered something under his breath, something that sounded like *so good, so good.* Thea smiled.

She moved with him, straining and grasping. He quickened his pace. He began to pound into her, so hard that the headboard bounced against the wall behind them. Reaching up, she pulled his head down so she could kiss him. It was messy and hot and wild, and she loved it.

He took her body like he'd taken everything else in his life. As Thea's orgasm built, she wrapped herself more tightly around him, like she needed him to keep her anchored or she would fly away into a thousand pieces.

Her release slammed into her. She let out a scream, her voice hoarse, her body slick with sweat. Anthony thrust one last time and stilled, and she felt his cock twitch inside of her. She smoothed his hair from his forehead as he came, tenderness flooding her.

How would she ever be able to let him go now?

CHAPTER SIXTEEN

Anthony awoke to the sound of singing. He thought, briefly, that maybe he'd finally died and gone to heaven, but why would he of all people have been allowed into heaven? Opening his eyes, he looked around the room, registered the clutter, and remembered that he was in Thea's bed.

And the person singing was none other than Thea herself.

He rolled onto his side, watching her at her desk in the corner. She was wrapped in a blanket as her pencil or pen or whatever it was she was using skipped across the page. She was drawing at—he glanced at his watch—five thirty in the morning. Yawning, he considered going back to sleep, but then the blanket slipped down to reveal Thea's shoulder. A lovely sight for so early in the morning.

He'd never acted this rashly in his life, driving for hours to see a woman. He hadn't even been this crazed with Elise. Yet when he'd realized that he couldn't let Thea go, he'd known he had to act. Anthony never sat on the sidelines: he was always in the middle of the fray, and he wasn't about to let something or someone go if he wanted it.

And he wanted Thea. It didn't make sense, and he might be losing his mind. But Anthony never said no to something that he wanted.

He'd been so confident of Thea's reception that her initial hesitation had genuinely surprised him. Sometimes confidence bit you in the ass, although Thea would just call him an arrogant son of a bitch. She wouldn't be wrong. It was his arrogance, confidence and drive that had gotten him this far. Without those things, he would still be a poor son of a bitch without anything to his name.

Anthony watched Thea silently, not moving, as he didn't want to spook her. He remembered how upset she'd gotten when he'd looked at her drawings back at the cabin. He still didn't understand why she kept it to herself. His business mind thought it was a huge waste of potential talent and, yes, revenue.

Thea could go far if she would let herself. So what was holding her back? He was determined to figure out what it was.

He yawned again, and Thea looked over her shoulder at him. She smiled, almost a little shyly, which just made him chuckle. The last adjective he'd ever use to describe Thea Younger was *shy*.

"You should definitely come back to bed," he rumbled. "Otherwise I'll get up and get you myself."

She smiled that smile—the one that shot straight to his cock. It was a mixture of flirtation and joy. It was such a pure expression that it seized Anthony's heart for a moment. But only for a moment, because God knew he didn't have much of a heart that could be seized in the first place.

"I couldn't sleep," Thea admitted as she returned to bed, crawling to lie next to him. She still had the blanket wrapped around her. "Sex makes me antsy."

"Is that a compliment or an insult?"

She laughed as she rolled her eyes. "A compliment, you doofus. Boring sex just makes me want to fall asleep, like listening to some professor drone on and on in lecture."

"Did you just call me a doofus?"

"Yes. Has no one called you that? Because I'm sure many have thought about it."

He growled, rolling on top of her. She laughed, and the sound was only stifled when he kissed her.

Anthony liked sex, for obvious reasons. He liked women, for more obvious reasons: their scent, their softness, their touch. He'd slept with a number of women in his lifetime. He'd even loved one, once. But he couldn't remember the last time he'd had fun with one. When was the last time he'd simply been playful and silly and even acted like a doofus?

He couldn't think of an instance, and for some reason, having that experience now with Thea scared him more than everything else that had happened between them so far.

"You're scruffy in the morning," said Thea as she touched his cheeks and jaw. "Have you ever grown a beard?"

"Once, a few years ago. But it was more upkeep than just shaving every morning."

"Hmm, I guess that makes sense."

Her fingers kept stroking his face, like he was a cat. He had to restrain himself from purring under her touch.

"I have to get my hair cut every four weeks," she added. She touched his hair, brushing it from his forehead.

"Have you always had short hair?" he asked.

"Just for the last few years. Believe it or not, it used to be so long that it was right above my butt."

"I'm sorry I didn't get to see that."

Thea smiled. "It was a pain to keep up with. I only grew it that long because I was lazy about getting it cut."

He imagined her with hair as long as Rapunzel, and inevitably his thoughts led to all of that hair coming undone from a braid before he took her to bed. It was an oddly intimate thought that once again sent a bite of fear dancing along his spine.

"Tell me something else about yourself," she said suddenly. She rolled out from under him. When he reached for her again, she slapped his hands away. "No sex. Just talking."

Anthony groaned. "I'm going back to sleep."

"No, no, come on." She climbed onto his side like an obnoxious kitten, although she was much bigger and warmer and curvier. Her breasts pressing into his side didn't exactly help him to stop thinking about sex.

He turned back over to face her. "I'll set my watch for twenty minutes," he said, "and then you can either get out of this bed, or more sex. Got it?"

Her lips twitched. "Is this a boardroom deal or something?"

"Yes. So, you agree?"

"What if I say no?"

He pulled her into his arms. "Then we can add twenty more minutes to having sex."

Thea sputtered with laughter, kissing him quickly before

sitting up. "Fine. Twenty minutes. Now, tell me something about yourself no one else knows."

"I hate radishes."

She hit him with a pillow. "Something interesting!"

Anthony thought, trying to come up with something that wasn't too intimate but that wasn't flippant, either. He wasn't exactly in the business of sharing things about himself. He made a point *not* to share anything that would render him vulnerable. Why should he? Making yourself vulnerable just meant people could use it against you.

"Okay, here's something. I didn't learn how to ride a bike until college."

"Really? How come?"

"We lived in the country, and it wasn't really a great place to bike. And I think my parents just didn't even think about it."

"I'm sad I couldn't see you as an eighteen-year-old trying to ride a bike."

He smiled grimly. "It wasn't pretty. I almost broke my wrist, but like they say, once you learn, you never forget how to do it." He tapped her knee when she was silent. "Your turn."

"I'm thinking. Oh, I know. I had a robin for a month as a kid."

"Only a month?"

"Yeah, I smuggled it in and hid it in my room from my parents. We weren't allowed to have pets. I can't believe I kept it secret for that long, now that I think about it. I found it outside after a cat almost killed it." She got up from the bed to rummage around in a drawer before pulling out a small photo album. She flipped to a page. "Here, see? Mr. Crackles."

Anthony looked at the photo of Thea and her red-breasted robin, mostly focused on how young Thea looked in the photo. She couldn't have been older than nine or ten, and her hair looked like someone had taken gardening shears to it. Her freckles were darker than the ones she had now, and her arms were red from too much sun. But she was smiling so widely that her eyes were almost closed.

"What happened to the bird?" he asked.

Thea's face fell as she closed the photo album. "When my dad found out, he took it out back and broke its neck."

He gaped at her. "Are you serious?"

"It was a quick death, at least. He knew we couldn't care for it, and it couldn't fly anymore. It wouldn't have had a good life."

Anthony stared at her, stunned that any parent could be so cruel. And that Thea could almost forgive such an offense. If Anthony's father had done that to a pet of his, he would've never forgiven his old man.

His parents had been distant and focused on working, but they'd never been cruel. After his dad had died, he and his mother had entered into a kind of formal relationship that involved a phone call on major holidays, a birthday card every year, and occasionally actual meetings in person that were inevitably awkward. But never painful—not like what Thea described.

Thea had set the photo album on the bed. Picking it up, Anthony flipped through the pages. When he got to the end, he noticed a name scrawled on the back of the last photo: Hortense Younger, August 1995.

"Who's Hortense?" he asked. "One of your siblings?"

At that, Thea snagged the album from his grasp, saying, "Nobody."

"Then why do you have a photo of her? Is she a cousin? Who would name their child Hortense?"

Thea's mouth twisted. "My mother would. My first name is actually Hortense: Hortense Anthea Younger."

Anthony tried to stifle laughter, but it came out as a cough. He started coughing, then laughing, and then laughing harder at Thea's expression.

"I'm sorry," he gasped, "it's just—that's such a *terrible* name. Why would she do that to you?"

"My mom had a flair for naming her children the worst names imaginable. All five of us have bizarre names." Thea sighed. "I went by Hortense when I was younger, but I started going by Anthea as soon as I could convince people to call me that. Hortense isn't exactly a great name when you're introducing yourself to your classmates. Then a friend nicknamed me Thea and it stuck."

Seeing the sadness in her expression, he realized that there was more to this than bizarre names. Her mother had committed suicide, hadn't she? And her father had been abusive. Thea hadn't had an easy childhood, and here he was, laughing at her.

He'd always thought his heart was made of stone. Except right now, that same stone heart was crumbling and feeling more than it had in a long time.

"I'm sorry," he found himself saying as he wrapped an arm around her, "I shouldn't have laughed like that."

Her eyes widened. "Did you just say the words 'I'm sorry'?"

"Yes, but don't expect it to happen again anytime soon."

"I'm not *that* hopeful."

She grinned, and he knew that all had been forgiven. She kissed him, and the softness of her lips combined with the lemony sweet scent of her skin made him forget everything. He didn't care about parents or pasts or names—the only thing that mattered was having Thea in his arms.

But to his annoyance, she ended the kiss to say, "Your turn."

"For what?"

"Another secret."

Anthony groaned. "Aren't we done with that yet?"

"Nope. And since I told you about my super secret name that no one else knows about…"

Then I should give her my pound of flesh in return, he thought wryly. "I can't think of anything," he lied.

"Nothing at all? You're so boring." Her eyes flashed, and he didn't trust that look one bit. "Have you ever been in love?" she said.

Not just one pound of flesh. She'll expect all of my flesh, organs, and blood, too.

THEA WAITED, wondering if Anthony would even answer her question. His fingers were clenched on the edge of her comforter, the only sign of his agitation.

Perhaps it had been unfair to ask him that, given his failed marriage. But the question had popped into her head and needed an answer. Because if he could fall in love once, then maybe…

She pushed that thought aside. *Don't make it worse, Thea.*

"I don't believe in love," he said finally.

"You got married, though," she pointed out.

"Marriage doesn't mean love."

Thea thought of the photo she'd found in his wallet. She might not be an expert on relationships, but she'd recognized love when she'd seen that photo.

"So you married your ex-wife out of duty? Money? But you already have money. Was it arranged?"

His lip curled. "Leave it, Thea."

"It's just a yes-or-no question."

"Why are you so intent on this?"

"Why won't you answer the question?"

"I'm not answering that question."

She huffed. "Why not? Are you afraid of being honest?"

"Thea…" he warned.

"Well, obviously it's freaking you out, although it shouldn't. So just say yes or no—"

"It's none of your damn business!" he burst out.

Climbing from the bed, he muttered under his breath as he grabbed his clothes from the floor. He started getting dressed. Thea's heart sank into her toes. She'd pushed him too far. She should've kept her mouth shut.

"I don't believe in love. Love only makes you weak," he said, not looking at her. "I thought I loved Elise. I thought she was the only woman in the world for me, and when she agreed to marry me, it was the best damn moment in my life. But I found out quickly that love is just what people use against you."

Thea didn't move. She couldn't. "What do you mean?" she whispered.

"What do you think?"

She swallowed. "Did Elise…leave you?"

Anthony laughed hollowly. "You really want that pound of flesh, don't you? Do you really want the gritty, messy details? Fine, here you go. I wish she had left me, but I found her in my bed, fucking my best friend. She cheated on me. She cheated on me for months, right under my nose."

Anguish and rage lit his features. Thea wished she hadn't said anything.

He said, "She betrayed me the worst way a woman could. And with my best friend, too. The only reason I didn't kill him was because she begged me not to." His lip curled. "Now they're married. Happily ever after, right?"

Thea struggled to breathe. She hadn't realized it had been this bad. Her heart aching, she got up and put her arms around Anthony, but he was like a statue. Unmovable and cold.

"I'm sorry. I shouldn't have pried," she said. "You don't have to talk about it."

He pushed her away. "It doesn't matter. I divorced her, and it's over. I've moved on. And I paid them both off to keep it quiet. I wasn't going to let them both make a fool of me to the entire public."

Clearly he hadn't moved on, based on the anger in his eyes. Thea wasn't dumb enough to say as much.

She cupped his cheek. "I'm sorry. That was wrong of her. You didn't deserve that."

His breathing was ragged, and she saw a flare of such pure need in his eyes that her heart flipped over in her chest.

He'd been honest with her. She needed to tell him who she really was. It wasn't fair to lie to him. But if she admitted what she'd done, he'd never forgive her. He'd never look at her like he did now.

Her indecisiveness meant that Anthony could collect himself. He finally pulled away from her, his expression now shuttered. Like it always was: walls upon walls upon walls protected this man's heart.

"You can't tell anyone about what I said," he said seriously. "I shouldn't have told you in the first place."

"Of course I won't tell. I don't blab people's deep, dark secrets." She tried to keep her voice light, but the attempt at levity fell flat.

Anthony just shook his head. "I need to go," he said quietly. At the door, he added with his back to her, "I shouldn't have come here. It was a mistake. I wasn't thinking."

She wanted to run after him. She wanted to tell him that it hadn't been a mistake to her, and she wished he would stop acting like she was some bad habit he needed to give up. But all she could do was listen as he drove off, taking him away from her again.

CHAPTER SEVENTEEN

"Thea, darling, sweet, adorable, ridiculous friend of mine. Unless you tell me what's wrong, I'm going to torture you until you fess up," said Mittens.

Thea tried not to smile but failed miserably. "Should I find that comforting?" she joked.

After much persuasion, whining, blackmailing and coaxing, Mittens convinced Thea to come out for drinks that Friday night. They'd gotten coffee a few times since she'd returned from her trip, but she'd avoided him because she didn't know how to answer his questions about Anthony.

It was hard not to be happy around Mittens. Currently, he had orange hair with red tips, along with purple nails with pink rhinestones glued to the tips. In regard to his hair, he'd claimed he'd done it because he was already "flaming gay" and liked to ruffle the feathers of the local soccer moms at various coffee shops. Fair Haven was progressive, but it was still a small town with small-town values. Mittens also enjoyed trying out different lip colors and had a bigger scarf collection than any person Thea had ever met. He was probably the most colorful person she'd ever met after herself.

But despite his flamboyant persona that seemed to exude nonchalance, Mittens was actually one of the smartest people Thea knew. He could weasel information out of anyone. Clever and witty, he made friends easily and enemies just as easily. When he'd declared that Thea was *totally fucking amaze-balls*, it had been a huge compliment.

Mittens pushed a shot glass toward her. "Drink up. I'm not letting you cry at Friday night drinks. I have my limits."

Thea drank the shot, gasping a little at the bite of tequila burning her throat. She bit into a lime. Mittens just pushed another shot toward her, which she took without hesitation.

After Anthony had left, Thea hadn't heard a word from him—not a text, not a phone call. And, yes, she'd given him her phone number this time. Guilt made her want to forget everything she'd ever done. The alcohol certainly helped to blunt her conscience enough so that she could ignore it.

Mittens had invited a handful of their mutual friends, many of whom were also animal activists who'd helped with the social media campaign against Anthony's company. They talked and laughed with gusto as the drinks continued to pour. Vegan cheese dip and chips were eaten so quickly that the waitress could hardly keep up with refilling their baskets.

Mittens folded his arms and assessed Thea. She barely resisted the urge to squirm under that all-seeing gaze.

"You're different," he said shrewdly. "And not just because you were stuck in a cabin with a total comic book villain and forced to kill baby rabbits to survive."

"No baby rabbits were hurt in our excursion," joked Thea.

She lifted her water glass. "Here's a toast to Sneaky. I hope he's sneaking around in some forest now."

Mittens pushed his glasses up his nose. At the moment, they were purple frames with diamonds in the corners, to match his nails. Mittens didn't actually need glasses to see, he just enjoyed the aesthetic. Thea wondered when he'd gotten them, because she hadn't seen this pair before. Or had she been too distracted to notice?

"So what's up with you?" she asked brightly. If she could get the attention shifted from herself and get Mittens to talk about himself, maybe she could get out of this night unscathed.

Mittens shrugged. "Nothing new. George wants to move in together, but I don't want to."

"Why not?"

"Because moving is a pain in the ass."

"You're such a romantic."

"That's why George is the one who gets to buy roses and shit on Valentine's Day." Mittens swirled his glass of merlot with narrowed eyes. "But you don't really care about George, do you? Or rather, I doubt that's the reason why you look so depressed and pathetic."

"You really know how to make a girl feel good about herself."

"You know, it's funny." Mittens took a sip of his drink and sighed a little. "In some bizarre twist of fate, you get stuck in a cabin in the woods with the one man we both hate more than anything else. The one man who doesn't give two shits about anyone but himself. I mean, that's an opportunity given to you on a silver platter to make a real difference. And yet..."

Thea tensed.

"And yet, you aren't acting like it was some great opportunity. You won't even tell me what happened." His voice had an edge of hurt to it, which only compounded Thea's feelings of guilt. Normally she and Mittens told each other just about everything, but in this case, she hadn't been brave enough to admit her changing feelings toward Anthony.

"There was so much happening, with him and the weather and Sneaky—"

"It's been two weeks, Thea."

She winced. When the waitress set another tray of shots on the table, Thea grabbed one and downed a third glass. At this point, it barely burned.

"I know. I'm sorry." She was halfway tempted to tell Mittens everything. He'd understand, wouldn't he? He'd fallen for more than one guy he knew wasn't good for him. He knew what it was to love and not have it be reciprocated. She was happy that he'd found love with George, though, who from all appearances seemed like a stand-up, caring man who adored Mittens, ridiculous hair and all.

Thea's breath stopped at the thought of love. She didn't love Anthony—she couldn't. She was just attracted to him. The sex was so good that it had muddled her brain. Struggling to find her composure when her brain was soaked in alcohol and filled with confusion, she'd almost forgotten that Mittens was staring at her, watching her every expression.

"I can take a wild guess what happened," he said. "You got to know him, or whatever personality he decides to put on for peasants like you. And he was so handsome and dashing that you practically threw yourself into his arms." He threw his arms out dramatically.

"Now you're just being mean. We didn't sleep together."

At least not at the cabin…

"Are you in love with him?" Mittens asked bluntly.

Thea shook her head, but that just made her dizzy. "Of course not. That's ridiculous. No, no. I know I said that I'd get dirt on him, but there wasn't anything I could find. He doesn't exactly share anything about himself."

Although he'd shared what had happened with his ex-wife just a few days ago, hadn't he? Her stomach twisted.

"Don't look like that," said Mittens in exasperation. "I'll stop grilling you. I totally get wanting to bang somebody who's hot but terrible. Been there, done that, wrote the blog posts. Fuck his brains out if you want, but don't forget that if he had the chance to screw you over, he would. Especially if he found out what you did to his precious company."

Thea didn't need the reminder. No matter what she did, somebody would get hurt.

As the night wore on, she drank until her brain was so fuzzy that she could barely put two coherent sentences together. She hadn't gotten seriously drunk in a long time. She wondered why, considering how nice it felt. Everything that had been weighing on her miraculously disappeared and floated away.

Actually, if anyone was going to float away right then, it was her.

Thea giggled. When Mittens raised an eyebrow, she just started laughing harder until tears sprang to her eyes. There was nothing inherently funny happening right then. It was just that she felt so delighted with everyone and everything.

Thea got up and slid into the chair right next to Mittens, leaning against him. He patted her on the shoulder.

"He's not as bad as you think," she mumbled.

Mittens voice was cool as he replied, "Who isn't?"

"Anthony. He's nice. He saved a rabbit."

"One good deed doesn't make all of his bad deeds go away."

Thea groaned. She reached for a glass of water, but most of it sloshed onto the table.

"No, no, you don't understand. He did it for *me*. He didn't care about the rabbit. He wanted to help *me.*"

She needed to make Mittens understand. If he understood why she'd let herself get involved with Anthony, if he knew why Anthony was important to her, maybe he wouldn't judge her. Her brain was too mushy, though, and she struggled to come up with the words that would convince Mittens.

She touched Mittens's face. It was smooth. Damn him, but he had better skin than her. He basically had no pores at all. How did he manage that? She needed to ask him what he used. It wasn't fair that a guy should be prettier than her. Was that sexist? She didn't know up from down anymore.

"You're a mess," said Mittens kindly. He stroked her hair. "Should I call a cab to take you home?"

"No! Not yet." At her exclamation, the rest of the table glanced at her. Thea blushed. "Anthony isn't the guy you think he is," she said in a low voice.

"You keep saying that."

"Because it's true. He puts on this…" Thea chewed on her lower lip. "Um, the thing that makes it so people don't know who you are—"

"A mask?" interjected Mittens dryly.

"Yeah, that. A mask. Because he's gotten hurt. But there's more underneath. I saw it."

"Oh, I bet you saw a lot of what's underneath."

Thea was too drunk to understand Mittens's innuendo. She shook her head. "He told me what happened. Did you know that his wife cheated on him? And it was with his best friend. She cheated on him, and he found them in their bed."

Mittens stilled next to her, although Thea was more concerned with finding a water glass that still had water in it. She was so thirsty that her tongue felt like it had dried up in her mouth.

"Who was his best friend?" said Mittens.

"Oh, some guy. Wait!" Thea found a water glass and drank half the glass in one gulp.

"He was his president. No, vice president. Board president? *The* president? I dunno. But he was pissed. I can't believe she'd do that to him. Or his friend would do that to him. What kind of friend does that? I don't get it. And then he *paid them off.* Crazy, right?"

In the far reaches of Thea's mind, a tiny voice reminded her that she was saying things she'd promised never to divulge. But then that voice disappeared again, like it had never existed. She was just trying to get Mittens to understand, that was all. She wasn't trying to hurt anyone.

"Huh, well, that's certainly interesting. I wondered if something happened. He filed those divorce papers pretty damn quick," said Mittens.

"He said I shouldn't tell anyone, but I knew I could tell you." Thea tugged on Mittens's arm, a plaintive note in her voice. "So you get why I couldn't help you. I'm sorry. I'm all mixed up."

Mittens took her empty water glass from her and handed her another full one. "Drink up. I'm taking you home."

Thea protested; she didn't want to go home yet. But

Mittens helped her up even as she batted his hands away. Once outside, she vaguely heard Mittens calling a cab when, to her immense humiliation, Ash and Violet exited a bar across the street. When Ash spotted Thea, who was now trying to skip but was mostly weaving around in random circles, he came over to her. He grabbed her by her elbow when she almost fell over.

"Thea? Are you drunk?" said Ash.

Thea laughed, then careened into her brother as she tried to twist from his grasp. "Duh," she said with another laugh.

Violet came up beside Ash. She touched Thea's forehead. "I think the term is 'shit-faced' drunk. We should get you home."

Mittens said something, Ash said something else, Violet said something to Thea. Thea ignored it all, concentrating on the streetlamp only a few feet away, its bulb flickering intermittently. She wondered why it hadn't been replaced yet. Weren't there bulb people to change them? How did you get that job? she wondered before yawning loudly. Lord, she was tired.

Soon Thea was being guided into the backseat of Ash's car. Violet had to help her put on her seat belt because her own hands were too clumsy.

Thea was drawing hearts in the condensation on the windows as Ash drove her home. Silence filled the car. Thea hardly noticed it. Ash could've been driving her to Antarctica for all she cared.

"What was that all about back there?" asked Ash. He was currently at a stoplight, and he looked back at Thea for a second. "I haven't seen you this drunk in years."

Thea shrugged. "I wanted to stop thinking."

"About what?"

"Ash…" said Violet quietly. The car began to move again.

"I wanted to stop thinking because I'm tired of thinking," explained Thea, annoyed that her brother didn't understand, and neither had Mittens. Why were the men in her life so dense? "Because I couldn't stop thinking about Anthony and I didn't like it. That's all."

"Anthony?" There was an edge to Ash's voice now.

"I hated him at first. Did you know that? He was an asshole. He's still an asshole, but then he was different. He wasn't who I thought he was. And then he shows up at my apartment—"

"He did *what?*" said Ash.

"Thea, you don't have to tell us this. It's your business," said Violet.

Thea, however, felt the words coming out of her without a second thought. What did it matter, anyway? Her life was a mess no matter what happened.

"He wasn't the same man I thought he was. He showed up here because he couldn't stop thinking about me, either. I think I like him now. I think I might love him. Isn't that weird? Can you love somebody you thought you hated?"

Silence once again filled the car. Thea hummed under her breath as she continued to draw hearts on the window. Then she drew her initials and Anthony's inside the hearts. *TY + AB*, she wrote over and over, like she could bring him back with each letter she drew.

Ash helped her upstairs to her apartment. She barely remembered him helping her take off her shoes before he tucked her into bed like she was a little girl. She giggled, because Ash was her younger brother, and she'd been the one to tuck him in when they were kids.

"Ash," she said, reaching out for him.

His expression was shuttered, but he sat down on the edge of the bed anyway. "Yeah?"

"How did you know? With Violet?"

He inhaled, looking away. "Thea, I don't think—"

"No, I want to know. Tell me."

Ash mumbled something to the effect of "when you know you know" before adding, "You don't really even know this guy. What you've told me already doesn't sound great. He seems selfish. You deserve better, Thea."

Thea yawned. Her eyelids were so heavy. She needed to sleep.

"Thanks, Ash," she said between yawns. "You can go now."

He squeezed her fingers. By the time he'd left, Thea had already fallen fast asleep.

CHAPTER EIGHTEEN

When Thea woke up the following morning, she was fairly certain she was dying. Her mouth was like cotton, her head pounded, and her stomach roiled. She stumbled to the bathroom and threw up the entire contents of her stomach, wishing like hell that she hadn't been such an idiot last night.

Oh God, last night. What had even happened? She remembered Mittens trying to get her to talk about Anthony, and she remembered drinking that third—or fourth?—shot. How had she gotten home? Mittens must've taken her home, although she didn't remember it at all.

After a shower and some toast and weak coffee, Thea lay down on her couch with a cold cloth on her forehead. She hadn't gotten that drunk in a long time. She frowned, trying to remember the gaps in her memory. Something kept niggling at her, something that she'd said or someone else had said. But then the thought fluttered away and she couldn't grasp it.

Afternoon sunshine poured through her apartment

window when someone knocked. Thea groaned, deciding to ignore the knock. The person just knocked a second time.

Thea staggered to the door, only to find Violet there. She had two cups of coffee, one of which she put in Thea's hand. "I would've texted, but I had a feeling you would've told me to stay home."

Thea sighed. "You're right. Come in, I guess." She returned to the couch, hoping that Violet didn't need anything urgent. Thea wasn't particularly useful at the moment.

Violet didn't sit, though. She set her own cup of coffee down and began to pace. The movement made Thea's head swirl.

"Violet, either sit down or leave. You're making me want to puke again," she complained.

Violet finally sat down. "Sorry. How's your head? Wait, don't answer that. I can guess." She rubbed her palms against her jeans before she said, "Do you remember what you told us last night?"

"Us?"

"Ash and me"

Thea's eyebrows rose to her hairline. "Did I see you guys last night?"

"You don't remember? Oh, I was afraid of that. Ash and I drove you home. On the way here, you said some things."

Thea grimaced. "God, don't tell me. Whatever it was, I'm sorry. I should never have drunk that much. I'll be nursing this hangover for weeks, I swear."

Violet nibbled on her bottom lip. With her blond hair and creamy skin, Violet looked like a model most days. It didn't help that she was tall and always well-dressed. Today she wore simple silver hoop earrings that Thea was sure Violet had made herself. Violet ran her own jewelry business, making every piece herself by hand, and had within the last year caught the notice of some major designers.

Thea had wanted to dislike her for simply being pretty and put-together, but it was difficult to dislike someone as warm and kind as Violet. Ash had made the perfect choice in falling in love with her.

"You said a lot of things last night," repeated Violet, her forehead crinkling. "You don't remember anything?"

"The last thing I remember is that last shot I drank. Whenever that was." She rubbed her aching temples.

Violet sighed. "Okay, then I should tell you what you said. The only reason I came over today instead of waiting is because Ash was about to break down your door, and then shoot Anthony in the face."

Thea groaned. Now her head really hurt. "Oh my God, I don't want to know."

"You said you slept together."

Thea groaned again.

"And that you might've fallen in love with him."

Thea swore and buried her face in a throw pillow.

"Those two things alone were, um, probably enough, but when we were helping you out of the car to get you into your apartment, you said something about helping hurt Anthony's company. That you were guilty and you needed to tell him what you did."

Thea didn't make a noise at that revelation. Her stomach dropped into her toes, and when she peeled the pillow away from her face, she saw concern on Violet's face. That only made it worse.

"I thought you were just talking nonsense," said Violet,

"but Ash seemed to think differently. There's been a lot of controversy around Anthony's company."

Thea opened her mouth to explain, but Violet held up a hand. "You don't have to confess, because it's none of my business. Not really. Although I guess I made it my business, didn't I?" She sighed. "I just wanted to say that if you've had this weighing on you along with your feelings for Anthony, then you need to be honest with him. Keeping things from the person you love never ends well. Believe me."

Thea wrapped her arms around her knees, sighing deeply. She could barely get her thoughts in order. "I'm a mess," she whispered finally.

Violet hugged her, which only made Thea want to cry. Except that crying right now would make her headache even worse. Sniffling, she just shook her head.

"I don't know what to do. If I tell him the truth, he'll never want to see me again."

Violet squeezed Thea's fingers. "If he cares about you, he'll find a way to forgive you. Or you can make amends. But keeping this a secret will only get worse each day you wait."

Thea didn't say much after that. There wasn't much to say. Mostly she felt embarrassed for blabbing her secrets like that, and she hated that she'd gotten her brother and his girlfriend involved in her life drama. She wondered if she'd said anything to Mittens. Her heart froze in her chest at the thought, but she would remember that. Right?

"I know you'll do the right thing," said Violet. "Drink your coffee, and I'll call you later."

"Can you keep Ash from banging down my door? And he won't tell Trent, right?"

"I'll try. I might have to tie him down, though." Violet smiled. "That won't be difficult to manage, actually."

Thea threw a pillow at Violet, not needing to hear about her brother's love life. Violet left, and Thea sat and thought.

She knew what she needed to do. She'd known for weeks. Now she just needed to gather enough courage to see it through.

ANTHONY POURED himself a rather large glass of whiskey and collapsed into his favorite chair in his office. When he'd bought this penthouse apartment six years ago, he'd thought he and Elise would eventually buy or build a house of their own. Maybe in Seattle, or maybe outside the city if they wanted more space.

He hadn't planned to still be living here after his divorce. After he'd found Elise cheating on him, he'd not only served her with divorce papers, but he'd purged the entire place of her very presence: from the pictures she'd hung on the walls to the random accouterments in her bedside drawer, to the array of soaps, lotions, and perfumes scattered across the master bathroom counter. Elise had taken a lot of her things. Anything she'd left behind Anthony had had his housekeeper toss into a dumpster so he'd never be reminded of her again.

He'd realized later that he could throw away every material possession that linked him to his ex-wife, but it wouldn't eradicate the memories. The only way he could get her out of his brain was to toss his own damn mind into the garbage, something he'd wished he could do on more than once occasion.

Now, Anthony sat in front of a roaring fire that only reminded him of Thea. He stared into the depths of his whiskey, watching the play of colors in the liquid. He tried to avoid thinking about Thea, but he couldn't purge her from his brain no matter how hard he tried.

He dreamed of her at night; he thought of her during the day. He saw her in everything. It was, to be honest, perfectly obnoxious.

After he'd driven up to Fair Haven and they'd had their spat, Anthony had returned to Seattle, pissed and wanting to fight. It had helped that the following morning, he'd had a meeting with his board, including his best buddy, Bruce. Bruce had left that meeting bruised and bloody—metaphorically speaking, of course. Anthony wasn't completely lost to sense.

But more and more, Anthony felt like his company was slipping from his fingers. He'd registered the looks of dismay on many of the board members' faces. He'd seen the smug smile on Bruce's when Anthony had let his temper show.

The thought of losing Bertram, Sons, and Co. would've terrified him once. Now, it just made him feel empty. Empty and directionless, like a ship without a sail.

Why had he told Thea about Elise and Ryan? He clenched his fist, wishing he'd kept his damn mouth shut. He hadn't told anyone that, and yet with Thea, he'd basically confessed everything. Why her? And why now?

Anthony finished his glass of whiskey and was about to pour himself another when the call button for his penthouse buzzed. He glanced at the time, frowning.

"Mr. Bertram, your visitor is here," said Alex, the doorman for the entire building.

Anthony pressed the call button, the speaker near the

doorway of his office. "I'm not expecting anyone. Send them away," he said irritably.

Silence. Then: "She says she needs to see you."

She. Anthony's heart seized. "Send her up," he barked.

He strode to his front door, and before she could ring the doorbell, he wrenched open his door to see Thea on his doorstep. He laughed at the reversal of what had happened last week, but it was a bitter laugh.

Thea looked tired, hesitant, and hopeful. The sight of her did something to Anthony's insides that he dared not think about too deeply. She seemed pale, but beautiful, in that delightful elfin way she had about her. In her hand, she carried a small bag.

"Should I ask how you found out where I live?" he asked blandly.

"It was easy to convince your assistant that I was a lady friend who'd agreed to meet you."

He grunted. He'd need to talk to Cara about giving out his address so easily. With an ironic flourish, he opened the door farther to let Thea come inside.

She tipped her head back as she took in his penthouse: the ceilings were high, showcasing the staircase to the second floor. Anthony wasn't much for ostentation despite his wealth, and after Elise had left, he'd replaced all of the furniture with neutral colors and simple lines. Functional, but expensive. It was preferable to Elise's love of rich velvets and deep colors that had irritated him after she'd left.

Thea walked to the opposite wall to gaze at a painting. She let out a little laugh. "This is a Henry Thatcher, isn't it?"

"It is. Do you know his work?"

Thea opened her mouth, but then she just shrugged. "We

studied him when I went to art school. He never did much for me, personally."

She wandered, like she wasn't entirely certain why she'd come. Anthony followed her without asking questions. But when she began to pick up a glass ball from a coffee table like she was shopping for her own apartment, he said, "What are you doing here, Thea?"

She tapped her nail against the glass. "This is pretty." At his confused expression, she added, "I wanted to apologize."

"You came all the way here for that?"

"I thought we should keep up the theme. You know, of showing up at each other's places without telling each other first."

Thea circled around another table, not meeting his gaze. He watched her, feeling rather like a hawk circling its prey, even though the prey had stepped into his net of her own volition.

"I shouldn't have said what I did that night. About your company. I don't know all the circumstances—"

Anthony held up a hand, stopping her. He slid an arm around her and pulled her into his embrace. "If you think I give a fuck about that night when you're finally standing in front of me, you're wrong."

Her lip trembled. Not wanting to keep talking, Anthony kissed her.

He groaned, deepening the kiss, and Thea melted into his arms. Triumphant, he slid his hands up her back to touch her bare skin. It had only been a few days since they'd had sex, but he needed her like it had been years. Centuries. He was already rock-hard. He was halfway tempted to bend her over this table and fuck her right then.

Thea turned away, ending the kiss, but she was breathing hard. He cupped her breast, feeling her nipple peak under the fabric of her shirt. She gasped.

"I need to tell you something," she whispered.

He kissed her neck, setting her on the table behind her and moving to stand in between her legs. "I don't care what it is," he said, and it was true. He didn't care. She could tell him she was the fucking queen of England and he wouldn't care. Nothing mattered but that she'd come to him and that she was in his arms.

Thea sighed. "Oh, Anthony," was all she said before she finally surrendered.

He tore off her shirt and bra, leaning down to suck one nipple into his mouth as he kneaded her other breast. Thea dug her nails into his shoulder, saying his name over and over again. It only made him more crazed for her.

But the table was creaking, and Anthony chuckled when Thea squealed as the table rocked. He picked her up with a grin that turned into a moan when she slid her clever fingers inside his shirt to caress him.

Anthony practically dashed up the stairs to his bedroom. For a flicker of a moment, he remembered how he'd found Elise and Ryan in here. The memory tried to hurt him, but with Thea kissing him, her smell and touch enveloping, he knew that the memory couldn't hurt him anymore.

Besides, he'd gotten rid of that damn bed anyway. And Thea would be the first woman to sleep with him in this one. All of his flings since Elise had happened elsewhere. The realization that Thea would be the first was surprisingly poignant.

Anthony flipped on a lamp before they undressed. Thea wore a black bra and matching thong, and when she bent over in front of him to take off her socks, her luscious ass in the air now, Anthony's cock jumped.

He kneaded her ass like he'd done to her breasts earlier as she stood up again. Thea wiggled her hips in invitation. He slipped his fingers under her thong and touched wet feminine folds. Thea shuddered when he pressed a finger inside her as he lightly rubbed her clit with his thumb.

She leaned her head against his shoulder. "Anthony," she whispered.

He rubbed her swollen clit harder until she arched and shook. She whimpered as he drew out her orgasm. She was so amazingly responsive that it only heightened his own need for her.

"Get on the bed," he ordered, kissing the side of her neck. "I'll be right back."

She shot him a sultry glance over her shoulder, and it took all of his self-control not to toss her onto his bed and slide inside her, consequences be damned. When she shimmied out of her bra, he swore under his breath.

"Don't move," he said before heading to the bathroom. He found a condom and rolled it onto his cock in record speed. By the time he returned to the bedroom, Thea was completely naked and reclining in the middle of his bed like something out of some erotic fantasy. With her breasts upthrust, her nipples a deep red, she made his mouth water.

"Oh good, you're back," she joked.

"Get on your hands and knees."

She shivered and soon she did as he told her. Of course, Thea being Thea, she made sure to do it as slowly as possible just to drive him crazy.

Anthony pressed his hand between her shoulders until her

upper torso lay on the bed. She was a feast for the eyes, and he was going to devour her.

He pressed his cock inside her, her tightness and heat squeezing him. She moaned as he filled her to the hilt. He stayed like that for a long moment, his toes curling. He couldn't get enough air into his lungs.

When he started to move, he could see Thea's fingers dig into the sheets. He gripped her hips, not letting her pick up the pace. He laughed, dark and low, when she cursed his name.

"Come on," she whined, turning her head to look at him. "Please, please."

"I love having you beg me." He just thrust more slowly, making sure to rub against her clit each time.

"Oh God, I hate you—" Her voice trailed off when he pulled out, waiting a second before pushing back into her. He continued that rhythm for a while until Thea's moans turned into squeals. Her sheath tightened around his cock, and he knew she was close.

His own control snapped then. He slammed into her, faster and faster, and to his delight she only pushed back against him with each thrust. His release coiled inside him, and right as Thea screamed his name, he came. His vision blurred, and all he could feel was Thea—her tightness, her heart, and most of all, her desire equaling his own.

They collapsed together onto the bed, both of them gasping for air. Sweat glistened on Thea's body, and he couldn't stop himself from licking beads of it from between her breasts.

They lay like that for a while, not moving or speaking, simply being. Thea eventually rose and went to the bathroom, and he could hear water running. She returned wearing his robe, which was so big on her that where it hit him below the knee, it went almost to her ankles.

"Anthony, I need to talk to you," she said.

Anthony yawned. "Come back to bed. We can talk later." His eyelids were heavy, and he just wanted to sink into sleep.

Thea shook his arm. "I need to talk to you," she repeated, more urgently this time.

He peeled open one eye to stare up at her. "No more talking. Just sleeping. Get into bed."

He closed his eyes, and when she sighed and got into bed beside him, he smiled in triumph. Sleep claimed him soon thereafter.

CHAPTER NINETEEN

Anthony was gone when Thea woke in the morning. His side of the bed was already cold, so he must've left hours ago. Yawning, she went to take a shower, the hot water clearing the cobwebs from her mind.

Her conscience pricked at her. She'd driven down here to tell Anthony the truth, and she'd failed utterly. She'd tried to get Anthony to listen, she told herself. But he hadn't wanted to talk. Then he'd kissed her and it had all gone downhill from there. It was like the second he touched her, every thought in her brain disappeared.

Thea dressed, sick with guilt and frustrated at how weak she was for this man already. Although it terrified her, she texted Anthony, saying, *We still need to talk. When do you get home?*

When he didn't reply, she hoped it was because he was in a meeting and not ignoring her. She wandered downstairs and got some food from the kitchen. After she'd eaten, Anthony finally replied. *Back late. Feel free to stay at my place as long as you want.*

Well, that was helpful. Sighing, Thea plopped down on the

living room couch. As she started perusing social media, her attention was snagged by an article that one of her friends had shared. The headline made her freeze.

Is this the end? Bertram, Sons, and Co. CEO cheating scandal of the decade

Thea clicked on the article with bated breath. As she read it, her anxiety increased with each word.

An unnamed source close to Bertram says that his former wife, socialite Elise Bertram (née Edgerton, now Elise Weaver), cheated on Bertram with her new husband. Even worse? Allegedly, Bertram used company money to hush up the scandal.

By the time she finished reading, she had to put her head between her knees, she was so dizzy. At first she wondered who had discovered this secret of Anthony's, but then memories began to flood her mind.

That night with Mittens. She'd been drinking. He'd kept asking her about Anthony. Thea remembered taking that last shot, and—

Oh God. She'd told Mittens everything. She'd told him the one thing Anthony had told her in confidence, and she'd basically word-vomited it without a care in the world.

Her hands were shaking as she called Mittens. She didn't know for sure he'd leaked the story. Mittens wouldn't betray her like that. He was her friend. Even though he hated Anthony, he cared about Thea more.

Right?

Mittens answered on the first ring.

"Did you leak this story about Anthony?" she asked in a quivering voice.

Mittens sighed. "Of course I did. Did you think I wouldn't use everything I could to take this guy down?"

Tears sprung to her eyes. "How could you? How could you use something like that against him? Against *me?*"

"Look, you told me the basics, and I had other sources corroborate it. It wasn't just you. You just gave me the first hint. Don't beat yourself up about it." His voice turned hard. "You promised to help me to take him down. You were the one who created that campaign in the first place. I'm not the one acting like a hypocrite here."

She couldn't get enough air into her lungs. "You were supposed to be my friend first. I trusted you."

"I'm sorry for hurting you," said Mittens, and he sounded sincere. "But sometimes you have to fight dirty. Trust me, this is for the best."

"No, it's not! This is wrong. He didn't deserve this. You don't know him. He's not a bad guy. He's made mistakes, and I hate that he does animal testing as much as you do, but acting like this is a black-and-white situation is absurd. And I told you something I should never have revealed. Don't you get that?"

Mittens sighed. "So you're in love with him?"

Thea stilled. Her mind whirled, denying Mittens's words, but she knew he was right. She had fallen in love with Anthony. She'd resisted it for so long that she'd been in total denial.

She took in a shaky breath. "How I feel about Anthony is irrelevant. You went behind my back and did this. Why? How could you? I would never do something like that to you."

"Look, if you don't get it, I can't make you understand. Sometimes you have to hurt people to accomplish the greater good. That's what *you* said, remember? To save innocents, you have to fight dirty. It is what it is."

"I can't talk to you. We're over. Don't contact me again."

Thea hung up the phone before wrapping her arms around herself. Her heart shattered, knowing that her friendship with Mittens was over. She felt like she'd been physically stabbed. She hadn't hurt this much since her mother had died.

Then her next thought was: did Anthony know yet? *Oh God, he'll never forgive me. I'll lose him and Mittens.*

The thought of Anthony hating her made her start crying. Losing Mittens was bad, but losing Anthony? That thought was devastating.

"I love him," she whispered to herself. And now she would never have him. She blamed herself for being such a blind fool. She blamed Mittens for his betrayal. Crying so hard that she was gasping for breath, she tried to figure out what she was going to do.

All Thea knew was that she had to try to explain things to Anthony. And to tell him about her involvement in that campaign before anyone else did. At least he didn't know that piece yet...

She fumbled for her phone, calling Anthony. But he didn't pick up. She called a second time, a third. She left voicemails. She texted him, but no response. Shaking with anxiety but refusing to sit by and wait, she grabbed her keys and headed to his office.

WHEN THE DOOR to his office burst open, Anthony glanced up from the email he was currently typing to see Elise storm in. She slapped a magazine on his desk before she demanded, "What the hell is this?"

Anthony picked up the magazine warily. When he read the headline, he saw red.

"Did you finally leak this?" Elise's cheeks were flushed, and her eyes glittered with anger. There was some satisfaction in her gaze, too, though. That was enough to make Anthony almost worried.

Slowly standing, he said calmly, "I didn't leak anything. It must've been one of your lackeys. Or Ryan himself."

"He would never. What would he get out of it?"

"What about you? Didn't you say that I could tell the world about your fucking my VP?" He narrowed his eyes at Elise. "So why would you even care?"

Elise seemed to waver before hardening her expression. "I don't care," she said airily, although Anthony knew she was lying. "But I have a feeling you'll care about the other details that were leaked."

She flipped to the middle of the magazine, handing it over to Anthony. He read the article, his anger growing with every word.

The details were so specific regarding Elise's affair with Ryan that Anthony knew beyond a shadow of a doubt who had leaked the story, including the most incriminating bit: that Anthony had used company money to keep them both quiet. Elise, despite all of her bravado, wouldn't have let this get to the press, and Ryan would never do anything Elise didn't approve of. Besides, that NDA Anthony had had them sign was ironclad. They were stupid, but not *that* stupid.

It had to have been Thea. The only person I told. But why?

The realization of her betrayal cut so deeply that it took all of his strength not to show it in front of Elise. He'd thought that Thea was the one person worth trusting, the one person who wouldn't fuck him over. But she'd used him, just like everyone else had done. How much money had she gotten, going to the press?

He tossed the magazine at Elise, disgusted. She scowled at him before she started laughing. It was so jarring that Anthony didn't know how to react.

"You don't know, do you?" she asked. Her smile only widened. "You don't know the best part of this whole story."

"Spare me your games, Elise." He had to get control of this scandal. He had to explain to his board why he'd used company money to hush up Ryan and Elise. *When Bruce finds out about this…*

Anthony could feel the reins of his company slipping through his fingers. Everything he'd worked for, everything he'd fought for—gone. In a burst of rage, he slammed his fist onto his desk so hard that it rattled the floor of his office. He didn't feel the pain in his hand. All he felt was the freezing of his heart at Thea's betrayal and the loss of everything he cared about.

Elise, however, just waited until he'd gotten control of his temper. Pulling out her phone, she handed the device to him with an email pulled up.

"I did some digging of my own. I heard about your little vacation in the woods with that woman," she explained. "You should read this."

Anthony was tired of reading. He didn't know how any of this could get worse. But as he read the email, he realized it could.

So much worse.

The recently disastrous social media campaign against Bertram, Sons, and Co.? The creators of it have been revealed. The masterminds include Milton Haverford III and Thea Younger, both of Fair Haven, Washington. Both animal activists, they created the campaign to take down this powerful company that continues to use animal testing. Shady? Maybe. Clever as hell? Definitely. Props to them.

Thea. Thea had been behind that campaign. And not only that, but she'd leaked his secret to the press. God, he'd played right into her hands, hadn't he? Had she planned them getting stuck together in that cabin? Had it all been a ruse? Had she fucked him just for information?

"Interesting, no?" said Elise. She was still smiling. "Yes, I know about that woman—Thea. It's funny, how many people who are still loyal to Ryan after you threw him out, who told us both what was going on with you and her. So, how does it feel to be betrayed?"

Anthony's mouth was dry, his heart pounding erratically. How many people had betrayed him? He couldn't wrap his head around everything being thrown in his face. "At least I didn't cheat on my husband," he growled.

"No, but you've humiliated me since that day. You never loved me, Tony. You loved your company more than you ever loved me. And this is the best revenge, because now everything you've worked for is being destroyed. The one thing you ever really loved—which wasn't *me*." She laughed, but it was a hollow laugh. "How does it feel? Because I can tell you exactly what it feels like to love someone who'll never give a shit about you."

Anthony moved so he loomed over Elise. In a voice as quiet as it was deadly, he whispered, "Get out of my sight. If I ever see you on these premises again, I'll throw you out myself. If I never truly loved you, Elise, it's because you're a heartless, conniving bitch. Now get out."

Elise paled. She opened her mouth to reply, but seeing the threat in his gaze, she backed down. Slinking out of his office like a kicked puppy, she grabbed the magazine and slammed Anthony's office door behind her.

Anthony didn't react. He went to his office window, gazing at nothing, feeling his entire world crumble to ashes.

There was a reason why he was a heartless bastard. Hearts only existed for other people to destroy. It hadn't been Elise who'd taught him that—she'd just been the introduction. Thea, though, she'd been beyond brilliant. She'd used him like a puppeteer. He could almost admire her for it if he didn't hate her so much.

Ironic, that the person who'd ended up betraying him again wasn't Elise. It had been the one person he'd thought would never do that.

He didn't move from that spot at his window until someone knocked on the door. Almost expecting Elise again, he was about to yell at her to get out.

But it wasn't Elise. It was Thea herself.

CHAPTER TWENTY

Thea took one look at Anthony's face and knew that she was too late. His lip curled, and when she took a step forward into his office, he said in a scathing tone, "Get the fuck out of my office."

"Please, let me explain. You don't know the full story. It wasn't me—"

"Really? I have proof that you're lying. But you've been lying to me this entire time, haven't you?"

Someone coughed behind Thea. Turning, she saw a young woman who must be Anthony's assistant.

"Should I call security?" the woman asked quietly. She shot Thea a wary glance, like she wasn't sure Thea wouldn't attack her.

Anthony didn't answer for a moment, and Thea expected the worst. Finally he said, "You can go, Cara. I'll take care of this."

Cara shut the door behind Thea, and Thea couldn't help but feel like she'd entered into a prison. Where had the playful, affectionate Anthony gone? Right now, she barely recognized the man standing in front of her. The mask he wore was in plain sight, and if he'd ever loved her—or even liked her—apparently it had already disappeared in an instant.

"Let me explain," Thea said again, more firmly this time. "You don't know everything."

"I would imagine I don't." His tone was sarcastic, and Thea flinched. He gestured at one of the chairs in front of his desk, a heavily ironic gesture. "Sit. You should at least be comfortable for this."

She didn't want to sit, because she was fairly certain Anthony was planning to wring her neck. But when he made a move toward her, she hurried toward the chair and sat herself down before he could carry her there.

He sat down across from her, like they were in some formal business meeting. It was so ridiculous that Thea bit back hysterical laughter. Why was she even trying? Anthony would never listen. He'd already made his judgment about her, hadn't he?

Thea refused to cower before him, though, because she hadn't leaked that story. Mittens had.

"It wasn't me who told the press," she said.

Anthony raised an eyebrow, darkly amused now. "If you're going to lie, you should at least come up with an interesting story."

"I'm not lying! It was an accident. I got drunk, and apparently I told one of my friends your secret." She grimaced, her cheeks heating. "I didn't remember doing it until this morning. It was stupid and childish of me. I feel awful about it. But I wasn't the one who sold the story: my friend did."

"Is your friend named Milton Haverford III?"

Thea blinked in surprise. "How did you know who he was?"

"It's funny," he said, ignoring her question as he rose from his chair to circle around her. He stood behind her now, like a predator circling his prey. "I didn't think you'd sell my secret to the press. You don't seem the type. You see, I wanted to believe that you were innocent."

He set his hands on the sides of the chair only inches from her neck. Thea swallowed hard.

"I wanted to believe it," he continued, "but imagine my surprise when I got to read a second email detailing how far this little farce of yours has gone. It started months ago. You and your little activist friends thought you'd topple what I built. You were behind that campaign, weren't you?"

Thea couldn't breathe. The speech she'd prepared in her mind when she'd driven over here dissipated like smoke in the wind. Anthony's hands inched closer until they lay on her shoulders, heavy as iron. His fingers dug into the tendons there—not enough to hurt, but enough to immobilize her completely.

"You and your friends were very clever, getting you close to me. How did you manage the cabin? That was a particularly brilliant bit of planning. Although how you could've predicted the bridge collapsing, I'm not sure."

"No, it's not like that." She turned her head, but he squeezed her shoulders until she winced.

"I wonder how stupid you think I am?" He sounded like he was asking himself the question. "Although to be fair, you played your role magnificently. Did you get a bonus for sleeping with me?"

Thea gasped. Wrenching herself out of the chair and out

of his grip, she faced him. "How dare you," she hissed. "You're making assumptions when you don't know all that happened!"

"I'm connecting the dots." He raked her from head to toe, disgust dripping from his expression. "I was totally convinced that you were attracted to me, that you wanted to save the animals. That you were innocent and good-hearted. But we both know that was a sham. Just be honest for once, Thea. I'm not interested in whatever lies you've concocted to cover for yourself. The jig is up."

"Will you just shut up? Will you listen for once in your damn life?" With each word, her voice rose. "You think everyone is out to get you, when maybe some people are actually just *people* who make mistakes. Did you ever consider that?"

He crossed his arms. "Fine. I'm listening."

Oh God, how could she convince him that she was both innocent and guilty? Swallowing the lump in her throat, she told herself that she could only do her best. If Anthony refused to believe her either way? That was his choice.

It didn't make her feel any better, though.

"I was a part of that social media campaign. It was my idea in the first place."

He sneered, turning away from her before she'd even begun explaining.

"I'm not done yet," she said, louder. His attention returned to her, finally. "I was a part of it, yes. I thought I was doing the right thing. Your company, this huge corporation with all of this money at its disposal, was and is torturing animals for profit. It's wrong, and I stand by that. Since you weren't willing to change, we had to do something that was underhanded. But it went viral for a reason, because people *agreed* with us. They saw the truth of what you're actually doing. Don't you think that's a real reason to make changes?"

Anthony went to sit on the edge of his desk, his arms still crossed over his chest. "If I made changes every time people on social media threw a damn fit, I would never get anything done. So you were behind this, knew who I was the entire time, and said nothing? How am I supposed to believe anything you say?"

"Because I didn't realize I'd end up lov—" She cut herself off just in time. She couldn't tell him that she loved him. He'd only think she was using that to manipulate him. "I didn't realize I'd end up liking you. That you weren't the monster I thought you were. Our time in that cabin changed everything. Don't you see that?"

"If it really changed your opinion, then you would've told me the truth. Dammit, Thea!" He pushed his fingers through his hair, disheveling it. "I thought you were different. That you cared about me because of the man I am, not my money, not my company. *Me.* But it was all a lie from the beginning."

"It wasn't a lie!"

"So you deny changing things so you'd be at the cabin with me?"

"Of course I deny it! I don't have money to throw around to make people do things like that for me. And how do you expect I'd know you were going to be there? Do I look like I hack computers?" She splayed her hands open, trying to make him see sense. "You're looking for conspiracy theories where there are none."

"No, I'm seeing where everything makes sense now. I see

where I went wrong. I thought I'd learned my lesson, but apparently not. You're no different from anyone else."

"I'm sorry," she said sincerely. "I'm sorry for that campaign. I'm sorry for lying. I'm sorry I ever let myself get involved with you in the first place. It was wrong and unfair." Thea drew herself up, refusing to cower in front of him. "But you expected the worst from the beginning. You think that people are inherently bad, that they'll only use you—"

"That's because they always do."

"They don't, though. That's where you're wrong. I was afraid to tell you because I knew this would happen." Tears sprang to her eyes, her voice getting choked. "I knew you'd never forgive me."

"Unlike you," he said, "I don't forgive people when they've fucked me over."

"Then that's your loss. Because people mess up—even you. And people deserve second chances. I'm sorry for lying. I am. But I'm not going to beg you to forgive me. That's on you, Anthony."

"You have some nerve," he growled, standing up and looming over her again. "You not only pull this social media stunt, but then you sell the story I told you in confidence to the press. And you're acting like I should *forgive* you?" He laughed tonelessly. "Why are you playing the victim when you were the one to blame?"

Thea's face flamed. "I didn't sell that story. It was an accident. I told you—"

"And I remain unconvinced."

"I would never have betrayed your confidence like that." Before she could stop herself, she added, "Because I love you."

Anthony stilled. The room seemed to freeze over, and like

that, Thea knew she'd lost him. Maybe she'd had a case if she'd only kept things neutral or logical. But love? To Anthony, that was a dirty word with only negative connotations.

"You love me?" His voice was silky soft, and Thea felt fear congeal inside her. "You love me?" he repeated. "So much that you lied to me? That you went behind my back to discover my secrets, to cause me to lose the one thing I've worked my entire life for?"

Although he never raised his voice, each word he spoke was like a dagger to Thea's heart. It was all she could do not to crumple at his feet.

"You're a liar and an opportunist," he continued, sneering at her. "I promised to take down the person behind that campaign. Well, I can promise you this: I'll make your life hell, Thea. If you think telling me that you love me will change anything, you're wrong."

"I didn't tell you to make you change your mind. I told you because I've decided to be honest." Thea lifted her chin, but she could feel the tears coming. Humiliating, angry, devastated tears. "I was stupid enough to fall in love with you because I thought there was a man with a heart inside you. But I was wrong. You're just a heartless bastard, like you said you were."

His eyes flashed. "Yes, I am. I told you that from the beginning. You should've listened to me."

Thea wiped her eyes, her heart breaking into a million pieces. She wanted to touch him, to kiss him one last time. But the quiet anger radiating from him was just another wall she couldn't overcome.

"You can hate me all you want," she whispered, "but I won't do the same. I hope you're happy, Anthony. I mean it."

He didn't say anything to that. She drank him in one last time—his dark eyes, his clenched jaw, the rigidity of his posture—and she knew this was the end. It hurt, but she'd said her piece. All she could do now was walk away.

So she did. She walked away and didn't look back.

CHAPTER TWENTY-ONE

Thea stared at the pile of folders on her desk and wondered who had decided to leave them there. Because she was one of the administrative assistants, her coworkers tended to think that her desk was everyone's desk. She would often find files, folders, papers, and all sorts of various office accoutrements that had appeared while she was going to the bathroom or out to lunch. They knew enough not to put them on her desk when she was sitting there, apparently, so they just did it when she was gone and couldn't object.

She sighed as she flipped through the folders. They were client files that needed filing, most likely. Already bored by the thought of having to file all afternoon, she put them in her drawer that she could lock, effectively forgetting them for now.

"Hey, Thea, I have some more files for you," said Jason, one of the newer lawyers Ferguson had hired. Jason was the epitome of the adjective *smarmy*, with his easy good looks and ability to talk down to anyone who didn't share his law degree from Columbia.

Thea hated him.

"I have to get this project done, so just leave them on my desk," she said, sighing internally.

Jason frowned. "These are confidential. They need to be placed in the locked file cabinet."

"I have a locked drawer—"

"And the key is in your unlocked drawer right above it?" He scoffed. "No, you need to file these immediately. I shouldn't have to ask you twice."

Considering that Jason wasn't even remotely her boss, Thea was tempted to tell him to go to hell. With a stiff smile, she took his files and placed them on her desk. She did it slowly, making sure that Jason knew she wasn't caving to his ridiculous demands.

"Like I said," she said, still smiling, "I'll file them when I have time."

Stunned, Jason scowled, muttering under his breath about how incompetent basic help was. He stalked off like an angry bear. Thea couldn't help but smile wider.

"He's such an asshole," said Nicole as she came up behind Thea. "Like he can't return his own files to the cabinet?"

"This is why we need to make everything electronic," said Thea. But with Ferguson at the wheel, who thought paper copies could never replace electronic documents, that would never happen.

"Hey, you never told me all about your trip," said Nicole. "How was it? Did you have a great time?"

Thea stiffened. She was surprised Nicole hadn't heard about the terrible weather, but then again, why would she? It was always raining in the Pacific Northwest.

Thea had to close her eyes for a moment. She saw

Anthony, the look on his face when she'd told him everything. The disgust in his eyes when he'd realized what she'd done. It had been two weeks since she'd last spoken to him, and every day she'd missed him.

She wished she could tell her heart to stop being so idiotic. He didn't love her; he'd never loved her. If he had, he would've at least tried to understand why she'd done what she had. She didn't expect forgiveness, but he could at least try to see her side of things.

"It was fine," said Thea. At Nicole's surprised look, she added, "It rained a lot, so that was disappointing. But it was nice to get away for a while. The woods were beautiful."

"You know, I heard this rumor that your favorite person, Anthony Bertram, recently rented a cabin in that area. Did you see him?"

"No," Thea lied. "I'm sure he had a way fancier cabin than I did."

Nicole pouted. "Damn, I was so hoping that you saw him. You didn't hear that he was close by?"

"No, how could I have known? I was in the middle of the woods."

Thea's tone was harsh enough that Nicole looked taken aback. Modifying her tone, Thea said, "Sorry, it's been a long day. I need a stiff drink."

Nicole patted Thea on the shoulder. "We should get happy hour on Friday. My treat."

Thea returned to her work, but she couldn't concentrate. She hadn't been able to get any real work done since she'd driven home from Seattle and had cried herself to sleep that night. The morning after, she'd almost caved and called Anthony, but she'd known it would be pointless. Besides, she still had her pride, even though it was in tatters. She'd said what she'd needed to say. What else could she do besides beg?

She wouldn't beg. That was too low, even for her.

Although she hadn't heard from Anthony—as expected—that hadn't stopped her from dreaming about him constantly. Some dreams were him coming to Fair Haven to tell her he didn't care about the social media or the leaked story. He loved her. And then he'd pull her into his arms, kiss her, and then carry her to bed.

Those dreams were always her favorite.

The nightmares, though, those haunted her. Oftentimes they were simply a rehash of their argument, except sometimes they ended with Anthony having her arrested. Or Anthony doing something ridiculous, like pushing her off a cliff. Or the worst one yet: the argument had simply ended with Anthony telling her that he hated her.

She'd woken up from that one with tears in her eyes.

It was strange, wishing to right a wrong when the one you'd wronged refused to accept that you were truly repentant. Thea realized the irony in that. All of her talk of forgiveness back at the cabin had come to bite her in the ass. It was a just revenge, when all was said and done.

Thea couldn't regret standing up for what she'd believed in, but she could regret not having the courage to be honest from the beginning.

And most especially, she couldn't regret falling in love with a man who'd she'd truly believed had a heart, even though he didn't have the courage to admit it.

Two hours later, her boss Ferguson stood over her desk with a grim expression. "Thea, can I speak with you?"

Thea was tempted to say no, but it obviously wasn't a

question. Rising, she followed Ferguson into his office. When he closed the door behind her, she knew something was up.

Ferguson steepled his fingers as Thea sat down in front of him. "I just spoke with Jason. He says that you were unwilling to assist him this afternoon. I told him that I would like to hear your side of the story before I make a decision about how to move forward."

Thea stared at her boss in astonishment. Jason had already complained about her? *That son of a bitch!*

"I wasn't unwilling, I just had other work I needed to get done first," she explained.

"Considering that I heard you talking with Nicole, I doubt that that excuse passes muster." Ferguson sighed. "Thea, I don't know what's going on with you right now, but quite frankly, you've been neglecting your duties here. I've seen you take longer lunch breaks that often stretch to sixty-five or seventy minutes instead of sixty. When asked to do something, you have an excuse about how you can't do it. Can you explain why?"

Thea's face flamed until she was fairly certain she was going to catch on fire. She hadn't put in her best effort, perhaps, but to get lambasted because one of the lawyers wanted her to be his own assistant and do whatever he said? That just made her angry.

"Jason isn't my boss. I assist everyone, but I'm not his assistant. He treats me like I should be." Thea took a deep breath as she tried to keep her voice level. "Just because I wasn't going to jump at his commands doesn't mean I'm a bad employee."

"I never said that you were a bad employee. Simply that your performance as of late has been lacking. To be honest,

Thea, your attitude is extremely off-putting. As an assistant, any tasks asked of you should be done with a gracious attitude. Instead, you insist on turning everything into a battle."

With every word Ferguson said, the angrier Thea got. "I can't believe this. I work hard. You know that. When have I ever dropped the ball on a project? Or refused to help anyone? All I ever do is help people!"

"Doing your job is one thing, but doing it with such a poor attitude? That's another."

Thea felt like her entire world was crumbling around her. It was ridiculous, really, considering how much she hated this job. It barely paid her bills to begin with. She'd never been respected here; she'd always been treated as if her lack of a degree made her stupid. Ferguson had never had her back, and he'd allowed his own lawyers to treat her as if she weren't an intelligent human being.

For a moment, she heard Anthony's voice in her head. *A washed-up wannabe artist.* Why was she so afraid of embracing who she truly was?

She stood up. "If that's how you feel about me," she said, "then I quit."

Ferguson's jaw dropped. He sputtered, saying that she was being dramatic and ridiculous, but Thea ignored him. She went to her desk and gathered her things. But not before she took those files from Jason. She went into his office without knocking and tossed them onto his desk.

"File these yourself, asshole," she said.

And like that, Thea was finally free.

She was practically shaking from the adrenaline as she drove home. Her phone rang more than once, but she ignored it. She'd probably done something monumentally stupid, but she didn't care. She didn't care if Ferguson never gave her a reference. Who cared? She wasn't going to live by other people's arbitrary rules anymore.

As Thea walked the stairs up to her apartment, she stopped dead in her tracks when she saw someone standing in front of her door. It was Mittens.

She turned to walk away, but Mittens said, "Wait, Thea! Let me explain."

"I don't have time for this."

"Just ten minutes."

She'd never heard her friend plead before. Curiosity warring with indecision, she sighed and let him inside her apartment.

"Why are you home so early?" asked Mittens.

"Why were you standing outside my door?" she countered.

"I was going to wait until you came home. I thought I'd better hedge my bets." He looked at his phone. "Did you get to leave work early?"

"Not that it's any of your business, but I quit my job today."

His eyebrows rose. "You put in your notice?"

"Not exactly." She sat down across from him in her living room, folding her arms across her chest. "But you didn't come here to talk about my job, did you?"

"No, I wanted to apologize. You weren't returning my texts or calls—"

"Why should I?"

"I know. I get it." He winced. "I can't say that I regret doing it, but I do regret hurting you."

Thea rolled her eyes. "That's not even an apology."

"You were the one who said that we had to do whatever it

took to get our message across. That the good outweighed the bad." Right then, his face seemed haunted, and Thea realized that her friend had lost weight. He seemed almost gaunt compared to the last time she'd seen him.

"I told you that story when I was drunk." Thea couldn't keep the hurt from her voice. "I should never have said a word about it to you. But you took advantage of me. So, yeah, I'm hurt, and I'm still angry."

"I get that. You have a right to be angry with me, but I'm sorry." Mittens smiled sadly. "I've missed you. And I know that something more happened with you and Anthony than what you told me."

Thea's face screwed up, and before she'd realized it, she was crying. Mittens came around and pulled her into a tight hug. She resisted, but she'd needed someone to comfort her. Burying her face in his shoulder, she cried—for herself, for Anthony, for her job. But mostly for her broken heart that she was fairly certain would never mend.

"Aw, honey, I had no idea," said Mittens as he rubbed her back. "That bad?"

"Worse," moaned Thea.

He sighed. "He's still an asshole, you know. But if you care about him this much, then he must have some redeeming quality."

Thea wiped her eyes, her face soaked with tears. She laughed a little when she saw how wet she'd gotten Mittens's shirt.

"Sorry," she mumbled. "I can't stop crying lately. It's annoying."

"I thought I was the one apologizing."

"You were. But I'm tired of being angry. I missed you,

too." Thea sighed. "I still don't get why you leaked that story, though. Did you really think it would make a difference?"

"It already has. Haven't you kept up with the news? There've been rumblings of a major overhaul over at the company. Of course, it's all top secret now, but…" Mittens shrugged.

"I know. It's a mess. Everything is a mess." She sniffled. "Why is everything so hard?"

"Oh, honey, if I knew the reason for that, I'd be richer than your lover boy."

Mittens stayed the evening, and they talked for hours. She told him all about her fight with Anthony, who she'd told she was in love with him. How he'd believed that she'd been behind the leak. Mittens winced when she told him that.

"I didn't think about that," he admitted. "Shit, Thea, how can I make it up to you?"

"I don't think you can. I mean, I could show Anthony the proof, but would he believe it? He wants to stay angry, I think. Because if he's angry, then he doesn't have to feel anything else."

"Well, that's deep. And complicated. But you can't fix everyone, even though I know you'd like to."

Her smile was sad now. "Even when I know I'm right?"

"Even then. People have to make their own mistakes. And if he refuses to see what he had right in front of him, then he deserves everything he gets, in my opinion." Mittens started smiling, a conspiratorial glint in his eyes. "Tell me all about how you quit your job. Did you burn down the office, too? Because if so, I support you fully."

By the time Mittens left, it was close to midnight, but Thea wasn't tired. She began to draw for the first time in ages, the inspiration practically flowing out of her. She drew for hours, feeling like the puzzle pieces were starting to fit together.

When the sun came up, she'd gotten close to finishing her graphic novel, the same one that Anthony had looked at.

Maybe she couldn't convince Anthony that she loved him. Maybe she'd never get him back. She'd have to put her heart back together as best as she could.

But that didn't mean she couldn't live her best life. She heard Henry Thatcher's words in her head, but they no longer resonated. She wasn't that insecure girl anymore: she was an artist who needed to share her gift with the world.

Thea started writing her query letter, not knowing if she'd ever land an agent for her work, but knowing that this was the first step to becoming the person she'd always meant to be.

CHAPTER TWENTY-TWO

Anthony stood at the floor-to-ceiling windows in his penthouse without seeing anything. In just a few hours, he would face his reckoning as the CEO of Bertram, Sons, and Co. He'd make his case, to persuade the board that he still had the right and the ability to run the company.

Anthony sipped his coffee. It was so hot that it burned his tongue, but he barely noticed.

He barely noticed a lot of things lately.

After the story behind his divorce, including his using company money to pay off Elise and Ryan, everything had gone to hell in a handbasket. The media had been pounding down his door, while the board had been in an uproar. Anthony had refused to talk to any of them until everyone had calmed down. He wasn't going to beg each one to let him keep his position. So, he'd waited, crafting his plan, and banking on the fact that despite this scandal, the majority of the board still liked him.

And who would they hire to replace him? They would

have a hell of time finding someone as capable and as dedicated as he was. Considering he'd been the one to build the
company himself, it was unlikely anyone else would compare
with his own work ethic and drive to succeed.

Despite all the arguments that Anthony should stay, he
knew that he was on shaky ground. Only a fool wouldn't
recognize that.

If he lost this company once and for all, he wasn't sure
what he would do. The thought was so distasteful that he'd
refused to truly consider it.

A knock sounded on his door. When Anthony opened the
door, there was no one there, except for a small package on his
doorstep. Frowning, he picked up the package. There was no
return address on it. Was someone trying to kill him with
Anthrax? It was such an amusingly morbid thought that he
chuckled under his breath.

He opened the package, only to discover it was far from
poison: it was a book. He began to flip through it, astonishment filling him.

No, it wasn't just a book: it was a graphic novel, the same
one he'd read a part of back at the cabin. He looked at the
envelope again and saw a stamp that read *Fair Haven, WA.*

Why had Thea sent him her graphic novel? He was
completely at a loss. Was this some kind of ploy again? If so, it
was a terrible one.

Anthony had tried his hardest to stop thinking about the
woman who'd betrayed him worse than his ex-wife had. Elise's
revenge had been petty; Thea's, however, had been calculated.
She had done her best to destroy the most important things in
Anthony's life: his company and his reputation.

But as the days and weeks had passed, he hadn't been able to stop thinking about how she'd pleaded her case at his office. Last week, he'd finally capitulated to his own insatiable need to know the truth that he'd contacted the journalist who'd written the story about his divorce. The journalist had confirmed that Milton Haverford III had sent him the story, not Thea Younger. In the journalist's mind, Thea had had nothing to do with it.

Thea had been telling the truth, at least on that piece. That realization had begun to chip away at the simmering rage inside Anthony. And even worse, it made him wonder: had she been telling the truth when she'd told him she loved him?

Sitting down on the couch, Anthony opened the graphic novel's cover to find a note written inside on the first page. He recognized the looping script immediately.

Dear Anthony,

I hope you're well. I wanted to send you this because I've finally reached a point in my life where I'm no longer willing to hide myself away.

You showed me that. Yes, you.

I hope that you're able to live your truth, just like I am.

With love,

Thea

He started reading without even caring about the passage of time. As he read the story of two star-crossed lovers on a distant planet, he became enraptured with the story unfolding. In turns funny, heartbreaking, and brilliant, by the time Anthony reached the end about an hour later, he wanted to go back and reread it.

When he reached the last page, his breath caught in his throat when he read the characters' dialogue.

Forgiveness isn't weakness, the female main character said, her expression both sad and hopeful. *Forgiveness is one of the most powerful things on earth.*

And love? her lover asked.

You have to be able to forgive to truly love anyone. Because none of us are perfect.

He could hear Thea's voice in his head as he read those lines. He read them over and over, and it was like the blinders were slowly being lifted from his vision. The anger he'd been holding on to—against Elise, against Ryan, against Thea—began to crumble and disappear. He could feel the burden lifting from his shoulders with stunning ease.

"I love her," he said, and the words both stunned and comforted him. He'd always known that he loved Thea—maybe he'd known since the moment he'd first seen her that night in the cabin. But he'd pushed the feeling down so far that he'd refused to recognize that it existed. He'd preferred to revel in his anger and bitterness, because it had felt like something he could control.

You couldn't control love, and that was the most terrifying thing of all.

Anthony flipped to the last page, where he once again saw Thea's looping script. All it said this time was, *I meant what I said.*

Hadn't Thea been terrified to show anyone her artwork, as well? But here she was, sending it to him. It was such a huge gesture of trust that it took his breath away. He didn't deserve it—not really. He'd been a huge asshole to her, refusing to hear her out.

She'd made mistakes, but so had he. He'd thought that she'd plotted everything in some attempt to take him and his company down. Yet that was only partially true. She'd fought for what she thought was right in one instance, and in the other, it hadn't been her truly at fault for his own story leaking.

He read the last page of her graphic novel over and over. He knew what he needed to do now. It was such a strange, but freeing, sensation. Maybe he could actually show Thea that he had a heart after all.

His phone rang. He distantly registered that Cara was calling. Glancing at his watch, he grabbed his coat and briefcase before heading to the meeting that would decide his fate for the rest of his life.

But now, he had Thea's love to give him strength. After this, he would convince her once and for all that he loved her, too. He'd never stop fighting to win her back. Out of everything in his entire life, this was now the most important battle he would ever fight—for the heart of the woman he loved.

"WHAT I WANT TO KNOW IS," said Bruce Weaver with a sneer in his voice, "how did this even get to the press in the first place?"

"That's not really our main concern," said Stan. He shot a glance at Anthony, who sat silently before what was basically his own jury. "I want to know why Anthony thought it prudent to use company funds to pay off his ex-wife and her—" Stan blushed a little before stuttering, "Her lover."

"Leave my son out of this," said Bruce. "He would never take money from the company like that."

"Your son, might I remind you, was caught sleeping with *my* wife in *my* bed." Anthony raised an eyebrow. "Ask him yourself if you'd like. I doubt he'd deny it."

Bruce spluttered, but one of the board members touched his arm. Bruce sat back down, although Anthony was fairly certain that given half a chance, he'd wring Anthony's neck.

"I don't care about the specifics of the story," said Stan, "but this involves the company. That's why we're here—not to gossip about people's personal lives."

"Yes, tell us, Anthony: why did you give money to your ex-wife without the board's permission? Let alone go against the rules you signed off on when you were made CEO." Bruce sat back in his chair, his anger changing to satisfaction in the blink of an eye.

Anthony thought of Thea's graphic novel, which was hidden in his office. He heard her voice in his head, and it gave him the courage to be honest for once in his life. Because he was tired of living a lie, and he was tired of holding on to something that had brought him nothing good. Oh, the money was good, of course. He wouldn't deny that. But money didn't buy happiness. It sure as hell hadn't repaired the tatters of his broken marriage, and it had only given him an excuse to keep apart from the world at large.

"I'll tell you why I paid off Elise and Ryan both," began Anthony. He stood up, slowly taking in each man on his board, each one who had a stake in the outcome of this company that Anthony had built himself. He understood why they wanted to protect it; in a way, he wanted that, too.

"I paid them off because I was angry, and I was ashamed that they'd betrayed me like that. I didn't want anyone else to know about it. That's the truth. So I paid them off and made them sign an ironclad NDA that only myself, those two, and my lawyer were aware of. The money included company stock, mostly, which was what Ryan demanded in order to sign the NDA."

Anthony gazed at Bruce as he spoke, watching the man turn redder and redder. "Ryan threatened to go the press himself, although knowing him, he was just bluffing. Letting the world know that he'd fucked his boss's wife wouldn't have been a great look."

"How dare you!" Bruce pointed a finger at Anthony. He slammed his palms on the table as he rose. "You dare to speak of my son that way when you're the one who stole money from your own company—"

"Stole is a bit of an exaggeration," said Anthony wryly.

Bruce's hand shook as his face turned even redder. Anthony was vaguely concerned the old man would collapse in a fit, although in Anthony's mind, it wouldn't be much of a loss.

"Sit down, Bruce. This isn't about you. You're only making yourself look like a fool." Stan's voice was like a whiplash.

Anthony had never heard him talk like that in all the years he'd known him. He was impressed by the older man's ferocity.

Bruce gaped at Stan, slowly sinking into his chair again.

Stan turned to Anthony. "Hearing what you've said, Anthony, I can say that myself and the board don't want to lose you. You've run this company like no one I've ever seen, and I know how dedicated you are to it. That being said, allowing you to stay in your role as CEO without any disciplinary action would be unwise. It would seem as though we condone what you've done. So we offer you this: you can stay with the company, but your position will be demoted. We'll elect a new CEO. That being said, you'll still have many of the same duties as before."

Where once Stan's words would've enraged and devastated Anthony, now he only felt...apathy. Yes, that was the world. He was losing control of the one thing that he'd thought mattered, but he'd been wrong. Wealth, power, position—none of it mattered if you didn't let yourself love and feel and want.

Anthony sat back down, considering his words. "I understand why you've had to make this decision," he began. "In your shoes, I would've made the same."

"Good, I'm glad you can see that we're between a rock and a hard place," said Stan.

"But I'm afraid I'm not going to take you up on it." When the entire board gaped at Anthony in disbelief, he continued, "This company was my life for so many years. I poured everything I had into it. It was like a lover, child, and a parent all in one. I only wanted its success." He smiled grimly. "But in the last few weeks, I've realized that this company gave me an excuse to be less than a man. I let it control me, and I let it push other people away."

He took a deep breath. "I'm resigning completely. Effective immediately. Because the funny thing I realized is that I don't need this company anymore. So I give it to you, because I know you'll take care of it. I have faith in you."

Anthony looked at Bruce then. "Your son was my best friend, and I trusted him. He betrayed that trust. But I forgive him. If you want to tell him that, you can."

"Anthony, are you sure?" said Stan.

"I've never been surer of anything in my life." He started smiling. "Now that that's out of the way—does anyone know an agent that wants graphic novels?"

CHAPTER TWENTY-THREE

Thea wasn't sure if she was going to die of excitement or nerves. Maybe both. Her stomach roiled a bit, adrenaline pumping through her, and she kept wiping sweat from her forehead. It didn't help that it was one of the warmest days on record in Seattle, with the temperatures edging toward ninety degrees and few places having air conditioning.

But Thea didn't care about the heat. She only cared about how this art show would go, and if she'd made a huge mistake agreeing to do it.

"Hey, it'll be amazing," said Mittens as they sat outside the gala in his car. He rubbed her back. "Do you need a Xanax?"

Thea laughed shakily. "No, thanks. The last thing I need to do is start blurting out embarrassing things."

She wiped her clammy hands on her pants as she tried to settle her nerves. She couldn't help but remember the last art show she was in, when Henry Thatcher had told her that her art was drab and lifeless. It was stupid that all these years later, his words could still affect her. If Henry Thatcher showed up in front of her right then, she would be sorely tempted to push Mittens out of the driver's seat and run Henry over.

"It'll be great," said Mittens again. "Come on, we have to go inside. I'm going to run out of gas just sitting here."

"You have a full tank."

"By the time you calm down, we'll be out of gas. Now, come on. We have an art show to go to."

Thea walked inside the gala, at first looking at other artists' work on the walls. She stopped to look at a gorgeous landscape in pastels that she wished she could put on her own wall. Other works included metal sculptures, canvases covered in glass and beads and ribbons, and more traditional paintings of people that were haunting in their colors and overall composition.

Thea hadn't entered in paintings, and now she wished she had. She hadn't entered at all, actually. After she'd sent out a number of query letters to agents for her graphic novel, she hadn't heard anything for weeks. Assuming rejection, she'd been about to send out a second round of letters to other agents when she'd gotten the email from an agent in New York.

Rebecca had asked to see the rest of Thea's graphic novel, and the rest had been history. Thea had soon signed with Rebecca's agency. Now she just had to wait for a publishing house to want to publish Thea's novel, but Rebecca was confident that Thea would get multiple offers.

The whole thing was surreal. And now portions of Thea's graphic novel were displayed for people to see. Thea took in one of her favorite panels, the one she'd written with Anthony in mind.

Her heart squeezed whenever she thought of him, which was every other minute. It had been over two months since she'd last seen him. She'd hoped that when she'd sent him a draft of her graphic novel with her note inside that he'd come around. To her immense disappointment, he'd never once contacted her and hadn't even acknowledged that he'd received her gift.

She still loved him, though. She'd always love him no matter what happened. It was bittersweet, finding success in her career but not being able to share it with the man she loved. Perhaps it was the price she had to pay for her past mistakes.

"Oh, Thea, these are amazing!" said Violet, pulling Thea into a fierce hug. "I'm so proud of you. I can't believe I've never gotten to see your work before this! It's gorgeous. I'm in awe."

"Thank you," said Thea.

Ash came up behind Violet and gave Thea a hug, too. Although her brother was hardly the type to give effusive praise, Thea could see the pride in his expression. Although the man that she loved wouldn't be here, it helped that her own friends and family had come to support her.

Trent soon arrived with a very pregnant Lizzie. He had to keep Bea from touching everything that she could get her toddler fingers on, which resulted in quite a few meltdowns within the space of two hours. Other friends and family, including Lizzie's siblings and their significant others and children also came, and soon the gala was filled with people.

"Look at you," said Mittens as he put an arm around Thea. He grinned. "You're gonna be a real star, you know that, right?"

Thea poked him in the stomach. "You just want to go shopping on Rodeo Drive if I get rich."

"Duh. Who do you think I am?"

She laughed, allowing herself to simply enjoy the event. Although she held her breath when strangers came to view her work, her fears were alleviated when she only received praise. Slowly but surely, Henry Thatcher's words faded from her consciousness. Her work wouldn't be to everyone's tastes, but that didn't mean she wasn't talented. That was something she wished she could tell her younger self.

"I'm sorry I'm late."

Thea turned to see her younger sister Lucy pushing through the crowd. Lucy lived in Los Angeles and was an aspiring actress. It was rare that Thea got to see her.

"You came!" Thea hugged Lucy hard before stepping back. "You're so grown up now! I can't believe it."

Lucy blushed. "Come on, I'm twenty-six now. Geez."

"Mittens, meet my baby sister Lucy. Isn't she adorable?"

Lucy disclaimed this adjective, but soon Thea was distracted when her other younger brother Phin came up. Considering how much Phin hated crowds and people and noise, Thea was extremely touched that he'd come at all. A lawyer based in Portland, Phin tended to keep to himself, always saying that work kept him from coming up to Washington to see his siblings.

Thea hugged Phin. "I'm glad you were able to come," she said.

"There are way too many people here," he said dryly. "Congrats, sis. You've really done it now."

"I have, haven't I? Now that you and Lucy are here, I get to introduce you to everyone." Although Phin groaned, he let

Thea lead him around until he finally told her he needed a drink and a break from socializing. Lucy, the extrovert of the family, relished talking to everyone. It was probably why she loved acting so much.

Thea returned to her work, noting that the crowd was thinning somewhat. As she turned around to get her glass of wine she'd set down earlier, a man said over her shoulder, "So you really did it."

Thea stilled. Her heart began pounding so hard that she was fairly certain she was losing her mind. It couldn't be—

"It's you," she breathed. Anthony stood in front of her, wearing a dark gray button-up shirt, the cuffs rolled up to expose his muscular forearms. But more importantly, she saw something in his eyes that she'd only seen in her dreams.

He approached her, taking her in from head to toe. She shivered, like she'd actually felt his hands on her body.

"What are you doing here?" she asked.

"I heard there was an art show. I thought I'd drop by."

"You thought you'd just 'drop by.'" Thea narrowed her eyes. "What game are you playing? Look, I know you're pissed at me, but I'm not going to argue with you in public—"

He shook his head. "I'm not here to argue." He laughed softly as he pulled out his wallet. Reaching inside, he took out a card and handed it to her. "I wanted to ask if you had a publisher yet."

"What?" Thea glanced at the business card, then stared at it when the words finally registered in her mind. *Anthony Bertram, Founder and Owner of Bertram Publishing House.* "Now I'm really confused. How can you run two companies at once?"

"Simple. I only run one now."

Thea stared at him, astonished, before guilt twisted her

stomach. "Oh God, Anthony, is this because of the story? You lost your position because of me? I'm so, so sorry. I never thought—why didn't you say something?"

"Because I didn't lose my place. I resigned."

Thea was fairly certain she'd entered into an alternate dimension. She'd wake up soon, and she'd be in her bed in Fair Haven, wishing that she could see Anthony one last time.

"You resigned?" She knew she sounded like a parrot, repeating his words, but it was like her own brain was incapable of coherent speech.

"I did. Because somebody sent me a gift in the mail." His gaze darkened, his voice lowering until it felt like a caress against Thea's skin. "Did you mean it, Thea? What you wrote?"

"Of course I meant it, you idiot."

"You love me?" he demanded.

"What do you think?" Tears had sprung to her eyes, and now she brushed them away irritably. "Do you think I quit my job and started showing people my work on a whim? I wanted to show you that I was brave. And, yes, I meant every word that I wrote." Her voice hitched. Embarrassed, she turned away.

"You didn't answer my question." He gently turned her to face him again.

It was as if the crowd around them had disappeared entirely. To her surprise, Anthony looked...unsure. She'd never seen that look in his eyes. Unsure that she loved him? He really was an idiot.

"Yes, I love you," she said. "But what does it matter? You don't love me. You hate me, remember?"

"Oh, Thea, you're so wrong." He wrapped an arm around her waist. "I do love you. So much."

"How? I thought you didn't believe in love."

"Like you said, I was an idiot." He linked his fingers with hers. "I had a few revelations while we were apart. I realized that my company was my excuse to keep away from the world. To keep anyone from getting too close. Yes, I was angry at you, but I know now that you were trying to do something good. What have I ever done that helped the world? I couldn't hold that against you. Not anymore."

"Anthony," she breathed. Realizing that they were still in public, she took his hand and pulled him into a semiprivate alcove that was technically employees-only. "Anthony," she repeated, before she started smiling like an idiot. "You love me? Say it again."

His lips quirked. He touched the tip of her nose before touching her bottom lip. That same finger trailed down her throat until his fingers splayed over her heart—the heart that beat for him alone.

"I love you," he whispered. He kissed her jaw. "I love you," he said again as he kissed her cheek. He kept saying the words, wrapping Thea in them, until finally he took her mouth in a searing kiss.

Thea's heart soared. Wrapping her arms around him, she kissed him with everything in her heart. Because the man she adored loved her, and she vowed that they would never part again.

After a long moment of kissing, they both gasped for air. "You have a publishing company now?" asked Thea wonderingly.

He grinned, kissing her fingers. "I know of the perfect first client. So, you never answered my question: do you have a publisher?"

"Not yet, but I'll have to talk to my agent first. She thinks I'll have lots of offers."

"And I'll win you in the end," he vowed.

She smiled. "But that's the thing. You've already won me, Anthony. Heart, soul, and body."

The love in his face almost blinded her. He kissed her again, and neither needed to say another word for a good while.

"Do you think he remembers this is his home?" said Thea as she and Anthony walked down the hill from the cabin to the creek.

"He's a rabbit. I'm not sure he remembers much of anything."

Thea elbowed him, but she smiled, too.

It was late summer now, and although most of the trees were still green, Thea noticed a few that had started to change for fall. Anthony had surprised Thea with a getaway to the cabin that had started it all.

At the moment, they were taking Sneaky back to where they'd rescued him. He'd made a full recovery with the assistance of the wildlife rescue. Thea had assumed they would release him outside Fair Haven, but Anthony had once again surprised her when he'd somehow negotiated with the rescue to have them release Sneaky to him. She had a feeling he'd made a hefty donation for the privilege. She didn't mind that in the least.

They reached the creek, the damaged bridge having been rebuilt since that spring. Thea found some bushes where Sneaky could hide out. Taking the carrier from Anthony, she set it down on the ground and opened the wire door. Nothing happened. Thea peered into the carrier, just barely able to see Sneaky's wiggling nose as he hunched in the corner.

When he didn't leave the carrier, Anthony touched Thea's arm. "Let's give him some space. He's probably terrified of us on top of being here."

They walked far enough away that they could watch the carrier, but far enough that Sneaky couldn't hear them talking. She hoped the rabbit knew he was safe and home now. She knew for herself that that feeling of coming home couldn't compare.

Anthony kissed her temple as she leaned against him. They didn't say anything, just stood there, watching, the sounds of the forest filtering around them. It was such a peaceful moment that Thea never wanted it to end.

After Anthony had gone to her art show and they'd gotten back together, they'd lived apart until the last week, when Thea had moved down to Seattle. Anthony had offered to move to Fair Haven, but Thea knew he couldn't run his new publishing company from the small town. She also knew that she needed a fresh start.

They'd moved into a gorgeous three-bedroom bungalow just west of the city proper, and Thea had fallen in love with it as much as she'd fallen for Anthony himself.

"Did I tell you that Rebecca got another publisher wanting my graphic novel?" whispered Thea. Sneaky still hadn't emerged from his carrier. "That's four places now."

"Five, counting me."

"Oh yes, of course. How could I forget?" She grinned up at him, which just earned her a smacking kiss along with a pinched butt cheek.

Anthony had embraced his new company with a fervor Thea could only have expected from the former owner and CEO of Bertram, Sons, and Co. But this time, he knew that the company came second to his relationship, and he showed Thea how much he loved her every single day. Sometimes it was simply a goodbye kiss when he went into his newly rented office space. Sometimes it was a bouquet of flowers when he returned home. And sometimes it was simply the way he whispered *I love you* before he slid inside her, reclaiming not just her heart, but her very soul.

"Oh, look! Look!" Thea elbowed Anthony as Sneaky poked his nose out of the carrier. She held her breath, and in the blink of an eye, Sneaky stepped out of the carrier and darted into the woods.

Thea sniffled. "I'll miss him," she admitted. Her eyes lit up. "We should get a rabbit! A pet one this time."

"I thought you wanted a dog?"

"We can get a dog *and* a rabbit."

"I have another animal in mind," he said, his voice turning low and seductive.

Thea raised her eyebrows as he embraced her. "Do I want to know?"

"I'm thinking along the lines of something that starts with a C—"

"Chicken? Cow?"

Growling, he pushed her up against the nearest tree, and

she could feel how hard he was already. As she rubbed him through his jeans, she added, "Cat? Chameleon? Look, Anthony, there are so many animals that start with the letter C."

He kissed her throat, licking her skin before biting down between her neck and shoulder.

"Camel?" she guessed. "No, wait, we should get a capybara—"

"Thea, do you want me to put you over my knee and spank you?" His eyes gleamed.

"Is it bad that I don't want to say no?"

He swooped down and kissed her, and she laughed before the laugh transformed into a moan. She tugged at his shirt, wanting to feel the warmth and strength of his muscles. His tongue glided into her mouth before he began to suck her lower lip.

She gasped for breath when he pulled up her shirt to kiss the tops of her breasts. "Cougar? Cheetah? Katydid?"

"Katydid starts with a K," he said as he sucked her nipple through her bra.

"Oh God, how can you remember how to spell things at a time like this?"

She pulled his shirt over his head as he unhooked her bra, and then they were kissing like maniacs outside in the forest. Soon he was unbuckling his belt, but not before he touched her, making her wet and desperate. He groaned as he felt how ready she was for him already.

After they got the necessary clothing out of the way, Anthony picked her up until her legs wrapped around his waist. Thea was absurdly glad that she'd gone on the Pill two months ago so they didn't have to worry about a pesky condom. Then again, she was so stupidly in love with this man that getting pregnant sounded rather wonderful.

Anthony pushed inside her, making Thea's head thunk back onto the tree trunk at the sensation of his hard cock sliding into her.

"So I guess you wanted a cock?" she joked, but it soon turned into a loud moan.

"I always knew you were perceptive." His eyes gleamed.

"You're so smug, why do I put up with you—" He started moving faster, and she lost her train of thought. He could be as smug as he wanted right now. She didn't even care. "Oh my God, don't stop, don't stop."

He didn't stop. His fingers dug into her hips as he filled her, the tree shaking and raining leaves down around them with each thrust. Thea clutched at him, kissing his chest, her release expanding inside her until she came so hard that she saw stars. She screamed Anthony's name right as he came, too, and they just held each other for a long moment as they panted and their bodies calmed.

Anthony gently set Thea on the ground, although she was fairly certain her legs were jelly now. They got dressed, stealing kisses from each other as they did so, before fetching the carrier and walking back to the cabin.

"We need to do that in every room," said Anthony as they went inside. He tapped his chin, a grin spreading across his face.

Thea shook her head right before he picked her up and threw her over his shoulder. "No, Anthony, where are you taking me?"

"We're going to christen your room, then my room, then the bathroom—"

She groaned, but she didn't mean it. She couldn't get enough of him either.

He tossed her onto her former bed before climbing on top of her. Touching his hair, she whispered, "I love you."

His eyes lit. "I love you. I'm so glad we got stuck together in this cabin. Even if you almost killed me."

"You deserved it."

Growling, he kissed her, showing her *exactly* what she really deserved.

Phin Younger had graduated from high school at the age of sixteen and had earned his bachelor's from Oregon State before he could even drink legally. By the age of twenty-three, he'd earned his law degree and had been hired by one of the best firms in Portland.

It had been five years since he'd graduated from law school, had started to work as a practicing attorney, and had entered the world as a well-educated man. He could speak three languages fluently (English, French, and German); he could remember minute details of cases that he had read about years ago; he rarely lost a case. He was, to quote numerous papers and awards, a brilliant attorney.

The greatest irony? Phin would've thought that by now, he'd be able to talk to women.

Apparently not. They tended to find his frankness and tendency to argue his point without letting go unsettling. The last woman he'd taken home had told him that he was "too intense," whatever the hell that meant.

He'd tried to be act insouciant, before realizing that

nobody knew what the word even meant. He'd tried to say nothing in conversations, keeping things light. But then something would come up that Phin knew more about than most people, and he'd follow that subject until the other person in the conversation stared at him in confusion and, sometimes, sheer annoyance.

So, no, he wasn't good with women. He was terrible with women. Women liked to be wooed. They liked compliments, they liked flirtatious comments. They liked it when you pursued them but didn't *pursue* them. Again, whatever the hell that meant. That advice had been given by his older brother Ash, the consummate playboy turned dedicated fiancé. Ash's advice about how to talk to women had never worked for Phin because Phin was the complete opposite of his older brother.

Tonight, Phin had been invited to happy hour with the rest of his law firm coworkers. As employees of one of the best public advocacy law firms in the state, Phin and his fellow lawyers worked around the clock, their pay being low and the cases oftentimes seemingly hopeless. But they'd all dedicated themselves to helping others who couldn't afford attorneys, the people who were most vulnerable.

But tonight was about letting loose. There were five other attorneys at the practice, all of whom were older than Phin by some years. At the moment, one coworker was laughing so loudly that Phin winced, while another seemed to down his drinks as fast as he got them.

The only female in the firm, Katherine, was closest in age to Phin. She was in her late thirties and married with two kids, and her no-nonsense approach to life and law had made her one of the few people Phin actually liked. Katherine didn't care about office politics or hierarchy: she cared about getting the work done, like he did.

"How soon do you think Dave will get drunk?" said Katherine.

Phin watched as Dave took another shot. What number was that? Four? "I give him six minutes," replied Phin.

Katherine laughed. "I give him fifteen. You're on."

Within five minutes, forty-five seconds, Dave was about to fall out of his chair. Katherine handed Phin a five-dollar bill with a grumble.

The happy hour continued for another hour before Phin had had enough. Saying goodbye, he ignored how everyone but Katherine looked at him like he was some self-righteous asshole for not drinking. It wasn't that Phin was against drinking: he just preferred to stay in control of himself.

Katherine followed him outside into the misty autumn evening. "Heading home?" she asked.

"Yes. Where else?"

"No reason. I just wondered if you ever went somewhere else."

Phin knew she was hinting at something, but it irritated him when people didn't say exactly what they meant to say. "Either spit it out, or I'm leaving," he said.

Luckily, she knew his ways. "I mean, do you ever go to a woman's house? Or invite a woman over?"

He stared at her. "Why?"

"Just wondering."

"No, you aren't. You have an agenda. Everyone does."

"You're so cynical."

"I'm an attorney," he said dryly. "Of course I'm cynical."

Katherine shook her head. "Look, it's none of my business—"

"So you're going to ask it anyway?"

"I've known you for five years now. We've worked together, we're friends, all of that. But I've never heard you mention dating. Now, at first I wondered if you were gay, or asexual, or both."

Phin waited, eyebrow cocked.

Katherine continued, "But I've seen you look at women. You aren't dead. And you've mentioned some women in passing. So, definitely not gay. But no matter what, you've been alone, haven't you?"

Phin wondered how much Katherine had had to drink. They were friends, but they weren't *this* close.

"I'm going home," he said again.

"No, wait! I just don't want to see you alone forever if you don't want to be alone." Katherine giggled.

Yes, she was definitely tipsy, Phin thought.

He smiled, but there was no humor in it. "Okay, let's get you home before you start setting me up on dates."

"That's a great idea!"

By the time Phin got home after dropping Katherine off at her house, her husband amused at his wife's inebriation, he couldn't get Katherine's words out of his head. *I just don't want to see you alone forever if you don't want to be alone.*

Well, joke was on her, because he wanted to be alone. It was easier. People were—complicated. He worked with them, for God's sake. He spent his time defending the people no one cared about. He'd seen the dark side of humanity, and he'd made a choice to keep himself apart. Besides, women didn't like him. They thought he was handsome, and they assumed he was rich, being an attorney, but when they saw him for who he really was, they bolted.

Phin told himself that being alone was the practical choice. He didn't need a woman in his life. No matter what anyone else said or thought, he'd live his life how he saw fit—and he'd live it alone.

ABOUT THE AUTHOR

A coffee addict and cat lover, Iris Morland writes sexy and funny contemporary romances. If she's not reading or writing, she enjoys binging on Netflix shows and cooking something delicious.